Landfill Meditation

Also by Gerald Vizenor

NARRATIVE
The Heirs of Columbus
Griever: An American Monkey King in China
Bearheart: The Heirship Chronicles
The Trickster of Liberty: Tribal Heirs to a Wild Baronage
The People Named the Chippewa: Narrative Histories
Earthdivers: Tribal Narratives on Mixed Descent
Wordarrows: Indians and Whites in the New Fur Trade

AUTOBIOGRAPHY
Interior Landscapes: Autobiographical Myths and Metaphors

ESSAYS
Crossbloods: Bone Courts, Bingo, and Other Reports

POETRY
Matsushima: Original Haiku in English

Gerald Vizenor

———

Landfill Meditation

CROSSBLOOD STORIES

WESLEYAN UNIVERSITY PRESS

Published by University Press of New England / Hanover & London

Wesleyan University Press
Published by University Press of New England, Hanover, NH 03755
© 1991 by Gerald Vizenor
All rights reserved
Printed in the United States of America   5   4   3   2   1
CIP data appear at the end of the book

The characters, scenes, stories, and construed histories
in this novel arise from imagination; any resemblance to actual
persons or events is coincidental.

Contents

Acknowledgments   vii

Almost Browne   1

Feral Lasers   11

Ice Tricksters   22

The Red Coin   35

Pure Gumption   48

The Last Lecture   55

Bad Breath   68

Landfill Meditation   98

Interstate Reservation   116

The Psychotaxidermist   136

Rattling Hail   147

Crossblood Coffee   155

Four Skin Documents   162

Luminous Thighs   180

Acknowledgments

The author is grateful to the editors who first selected these stories for publication. Lawrence Smith published "Feral Lasers" in *Caliban 6*. The "Ice Tricksters" appeared as "Almost a Whole Trickster" in *A Gathering of Flowers*, edited by Joyce Carol Thomas, Harper & Row. "Almost Browne" was selected by the PEN Syndicated Fiction Project for newspaper and radio distribution. "Pure Gumption" and "The Last Lecture" were first published in *The Trickster of Liberty*, University of Minnesota Press.

"Interstate Reservation" was published as "Episodes in Mythic Verism" in *The New Native American Novel*, University of New Mexico Press. "Bad Breath" appeared in *An Illuminated History of the Future*, edited by Curtis White, Fiction Collective Two.

"Crossblood Coffee" was first published as "Anishinabica: Instant Tribal Coffee" in the *Minneapolis Star* and later as "Reservation Café: The Origins of American Indian Instant Coffee" in *Earth Power Coming*, Navajo Community College Press. "Landfill Meditation," the title story, was first published in the *Minneapolis Star* and later, with "The Psychotaxidermist" and "Rattling Hail," in *Words in the Blood*, New American Library.

"Four Skin Documents" was published in *Tamaqua*; an earlier version appeared as "Word Cinemas" in a special edition of

Book Forum, edited by Elaine Jahner. "Luminous Thighs" was first published in *Genre*, The University of Oklahoma. "The Red Coin" is published here for the first time.

March 1991   G. V.

Landfill Meditation

Almost Browne

ALMOST BROWNE was born on the White Earth Indian Reservation in Minnesota. Well, he was *almost* born there; that much is the absolute truth about his birth. Almost, you see, is a crossblood and he was born on the road; his father is tribal and his mother is blonde.

Marthie Jean Peterson and Hare Browne met on the dock at Sugar Bush Lake. He worked for the conservation department on the reservation, and she was there on vacation with her parents. Marthie Jean trusted her heart and proposed in the back of an aluminum boat. Hare was silent, but they were married that year at the end of the wild rice season.

Hare and Marthie had been in the cities over the weekend with her relatives. The men told stories about fish farms, construction, the weather, and automobiles, and the women prepared five meals that were eaten in front of the television set in the amusement room.

Marthie loved fish sticks and baloney, but most of all she loved to eat orange Jell-O with mayonnaise. She had just finished a second bowl when she felt the first birth pain.

"Hare, your son is almost here," she whispered in his ear. Marthie did not want her parents to know about the pain; naturally, they never would have allowed her to return to the reservation in labor.

Marthie never forgot anything; even as a child she could recite the state capitals. She remembered birthdates and presidents, but that afternoon she packed two baloney sandwiches and forgot her purse. She was on the road in labor with no checkbook, no money, no proof of identity. She was in love and trusted her heart.

The leaves had turned earlier than usual that autumn, and the silent crows bounced on the cold black road a few miles this side of the reservation border. Ahead, the red sumac burned on the curve.

Hare was worried that the crows would not move in time, so he slowed down and honked the horn. The crows circled a dead squirrel. He honked again, but the crows were too wise to be threatened. The engine wheezed, lurched three times, and then died on the curve in the light of the sumac.

Almost earned his nickname in the back seat of that seventeen-year-old hatchback; he was born on the road, almost on the reservation. His father pushed the car around the curve, past the crows and red sumac, about a half a mile to a small town. There, closer to the reservation border, he borrowed two gallons of gas from the station manager and hurried to the hospital on the White Earth Reservation.

The hatchback thundered over the unpaved government road; a wild bloom of brown dust covered the birch on the shoulders. The dust shrouded the red arrow to the resort at Sugar Bush Lake. The hospital was located at the end of the road near the federal water tower.

Wolfie Wight, the reservation medical doctor, opened the hatchback and reached into the dust. Her enormous head, wide grin, and hard pink hands frightened the crossblood infant in the back seat.

Almost was covered with dust, darker at birth than he has ever been since then. Wolfie laughed when the child turned white in his first bath. He was weighed and measured, and a tribal nurse listened to his heartbeat. Later, the doctor raised her enormous black fountain pen over the birth certificate and asked the parents, "Where was your child born?"

"White Earth," shouted the father.

"Hatchback?" The doctor smiled.

"White Earth," he answered, uncertain of his rights.

"Hatchback near the reservation?"

"White Earth," said the father a third time.

"Almost White Earth," said the doctor.

"White Earth," he repeated, determined that the birth of his son would be recorded on the reservation. He was born so close to the border, and he never touched the earth outside the reservation.

"Indeed, Almost Browne," said the doctor, and printed that name on the birth certificate. Wolfie recorded the place of birth as "Hatchback at White Earth" and signed the certificate with a flourish. "One more trail born halfbreed with a new name," she told the nurse. The nurse was silent; she resisted medical humor about tribal people.

Almost was born to be a tribal trickster. He learned to walk and talk in the wild brush; he listened to birds, water, lightning, the crack of thunder and ice, the turn of seasons; and he moved with animals in dreams. But he was more at home on cracked polyvinyl chloride in the back seats of cars, a natural outcome of his birth in a used hatchback.

Almost told a blonde anthropologist one summer that he

was born in the bottom of a boat and learned how to read in limousines; she was amused and recorded his stories in narrow blue notebooks. They sat in the back seat of an abandoned car.

"I grew up with mongrels," he told the anthropologist. "We lived in seven cars, dead ones, behind the house. One car, the brown one, that was my observatory. That's where I made the summer star charts."

"Indian constellations?" asked the anthropologist.

"Yes, the stars that moved in the sunroof," he explained. "I marked the stars on cards, the bright ones that came into the sunroof got names."

"What were the names?" asked the anthropologist.

"The sunroof stars."

"The names of the constellations?"

"We had nicknames," he answered.

"What were the names?"

"The sunroof charts were like cartoon pictures."

"What names?"

"Moths are on one chart."

"What are the other names?"

"Mosquitoes, white lies, pure gumption, private jones."

"Those are constellations?"

"The sunroof charts are named after my dogs," he said and called the mongrels into the back seat. White Lies licked the blond hair on the arms of the anthropologist.

Almost learned how to read from books that had been burned in a fire at the reservation library. The books were burned on the sides. He read the centers of the pages and imagined the stories from the words that were burned.

Almost had one close friend; his nickname was Drain. They were so close that some people thought they must be brothers. The two were born on the same day near the same town on the reservation border. Drain lived on a farm, the fifth son of white immigrants.

Drain was a reservation consumer, because he believed the stories he heard about the tribe. He became what he heard, and when the old men told him to shout, he shouted; he learned to shout at shadows and thunderstorms.

Almost told stories that made the tribe seem more real; he imagined a trickster world of chance and transformation. Drain listened and consumed the adventures. The two were inseparable; one the crossblood trickster, the other a white consumer. Together, the reservation became their paradise in stories.

Almost never attended school; well, he almost never attended. He lived on the border between two school districts, one white and the other tribal. When he wanted to use the machines in school, the microscopes, lathes, and laboratories, he would attend classes, but not more than two or three times a month. Each school thought he attended the other, and besides, no one cared that much where he lived or what he learned.

Almost learned four natural deals about life from his grandmother; he learned to see the wild world as deals between memories and tribal stories. The first deal, she told him, was chance, where things just happen and that becomes the deal with animals and their languages; words were pictures in the second natural deal; the third deal, she said, was to eat from the real world, not from the pictures on menus; and the last deal, she told him, was to liberate his mind with trickster stories.

"In natural deals," he explained to his best friend, "we act, bargain, agree, deliver, and remember that birds never eat monarchs in our stories."

"What monarchs?" asked Drain.

"The milkweed butterflies."

"So, what's the deal?"

"We're the deal in our stories."

"Some deal," moaned Drain.

"The deal is that whites are fleas and the tribes are the best dealers," said Almost. "Indians are the tricksters, we are the rabbits, and when we get excited, our ears heat up and the white fleas breed."

Almost converted a reservation station wagon into a bookmobile; he sold books from a rack that unfolded out of the back. The books, however, were not what most people expected, not even in trickster stories, and he needed a loan to expand his business.

"We're almost a bookstore," said Almost.

"Blank books?" shouted Wolfie. "You can't sell books on a reservation, people don't read here, not even blank ones."

"Some of them are burned," said Almost.

"You're crazy, blank and burned books," said the doctor, "but you do have gumption, that much is worth a loan." She polished her black pen on the sleeve of her white coat and signed a check to the crossblood.

Almost the whole truth:

Almost is my name, my real name, believe that or not, because my father ran out of money and then out of gas on the way back. I was born in the back seat of a beatup reservation car, almost white, almost on the reservation, and almost a real person.

White Jaws, the government doctor who got her cold hands on my birth certificate, gave me my name. Imagine, if we had run out of gas ten miles earlier, near a white hospital, my name might be Robert, or how about Truman? Instead, White Jaws made me Almost.

Listen, there must be something to learn in public schools,

but not by me. My imagination stopped at the double doors; being inside a school was like a drain on my brain. So, my chance to learn came in bad nature and white books. Not picture nature in a dozen bird names, but road kills, white pine in eagle nests, fleas in rabbit ears, the last green flies in late autumn, and moths that whisper, whisper at the mirror. Nature voices, crows in the poplars, not plastic bird mobiles over a baby crib. So, nature was my big book, imagination was my teacher.

Classrooms were nothing more than parking lots to me, places to park a mind rather than drive a mind wild in the glorious woods, through the dangerous present in the winter when the whole real world struggles to survive. For me, double doors and desks are the end of imagination, the end of animals, the end of nature, and the end of the tribes. I might never have entered the book business if I had been forced to attend a white school.

The truth is, I almost got into the book business before my time. A blonde anthropology student started a library on the reservation and she put me in charge of finding and sorting books. I found hundreds of books that summer, what a great time, books were like chance meetings, but the whole thing burned down before I learned how to read. The anthropologist told me not to use my finger on the page but we never practiced in any real books. She talked and talked and then when the building burned down she drove back home to the city. People always come here with some other place in mind.

Drain, he's my best friend, said it was a good thing the library burned because most of the stuff in there was worthless digest books that nobody wanted to read in the first place. Drain is a white farm kid who lives on the other side of the road, on the white side of the road, outside the reservation. He learned how to read in another language before he went to school.

I actually taught myself how to read with almost whole books, and that's the truth. I'd read with my finger first, word for word out loud right down to the burned parts and then I'd picture the rest, or imagine the rest of the words on the page. The words became more real in my imagination. From the words in pictures I turned back to the words on the center of the page. Finally, I could imagine the words and read the whole page, printed or burned.

Listen, there are words almost everywhere. I realized that in a chance moment. Words are in the air, in our blood, words were always there, way before my burned book collection in the back seat of a car. Words are in snow, trees, leaves, wind, birds, beaver, the sound of ice cracking; words are in fish and mongrels, where they've been since we came to this place with the animals. My winter breath is a word, we are words, real words, and the mongrels are their own words. Words are crossbloods too, almost whole right down to the cold printed page burned on the sides.

Drain never thought about real words because he found them in books, nowhere else. He taught me how to read better, and I showed him how to see real words where we lived, and the words that were burned on the pages of my books. Words burned but never dead. It was my idea to open a bookstore with blank books, a mobile bookstore.

Doctor Wolfie gave us a loan, so we packed up and drove to the city, where we started our blank book business near the university. Drain somehow knew the city like the back of his hand. I told him that was the same as finding words in animals. Everything was almost perfect; we were making good money on the street and going to parties with college students, but then the university police arrested us for false advertising, fraud, and trading on the campus without a permit. The car wasn't registered, and we didn't have a license. I think that was the real problem.

Drain played Indian because the judge said he would drop the charges if we went straight back to the reservation where we belonged and learned a useful trade.

"Almost Browne, that's my real name," I told the judge. "I was almost born in the city." The judge never even smiled. These men who rule words from behind double doors and polished benches miss the best words in the language, they miss the real words. They never hear the real words in court, not even the burned words. No one would ever bring real words to court.

Drain was bold and determined in the city. He drove right onto campus, opened the back of the station wagon, unfolded our book rack, and we were in business. That's how it happened, but the judge was not even listening. Wait, we played a shaman drum tape on a small recorder perched on the top of the car. The tape was old; the sound crackled like a pine fire, we told the judge.

Professor Monte Franzgomery was always there, every day. He would dance a little to the music, and he helped us sell blank books to college students. "Listen to that music," he shouted at the students. "That's real music, ethnic authenticity at the very threshold of civilization." That old professor shouted that we were real too, but we were never sure about him because he talked too much. We knew we were on the threshold of something big when we sold out our whole stock in a week, more than a hundred blank books in a week.

Monte said our blank books made more sense to him than anything he had ever read. This guy was really cracked. Our books were blank except on one page there was an original tribal pictomyth painted by me in green ink, a different pictomyth on a different page in every blank book. Yes, pictomyths, stories that are imagined about a picture, about memories. So, even our blank books had a story. I think those college students were tired of books filled with words behind double doors that never pictured anything. Our blank books said everything, whatever you could imagine in a picture. One pictomyth was almost worth a good story in those days.

Well, we were almost on our way to a fortune at the university when the police burned our blank books. Not really, but a ban on the sale of blank books is almost as bad as burning a book with print.

So, now we're back on the reservation in the mail-order business, a sovereign tribal blank book business in an abandoned car. Our business has been brisk, almost as good as it was at the university; better yet, there's no overhead in the back seat of a station wagon on the reservation. Listen, last week the best edition of our blank books was adopted in a cinema class at the University of California in Santa Cruz. Blank books are real popular on the coast.

Monte promised that he would use our blank books in his seminar on romantic literature. He told a newspaper reporter, when we were arrested, that the pictomyths were a "spontaneous overflow of powerful feelings."

Drain said we should autograph our blank books, a different signature on each book. I told him the pictomyths were enough. No, he said, the consumer wants something new, something different from time to time. The stories in the pictomyths are what's new, I told him. He was right, and we agreed. I made pictures and he signed the books. He even signed the names of tribal leaders, presidents, and famous authors.

Later, we published oversized blank books, and a miniature edition of blank books. Drain bought a new car, we did almost everything with blank books. We even started a blank book library on the reservation, but that's another story for another time.

Feral Lasers

ALMOST BROWNE was born twice, the sublime measure of a crossblood trickster. His parents, a tribal father and a white mother, had been in the cities and ran out of gas on the way back to deliver their first son on the White Earth Reservation in Minnesota.

Almost earned his nickname in the back seat of a seventeen-year-old hatchback. The leaves had turned, the wind was cold. Two crows bounced on the road, an auspicious chorus near the tribal border.

Father Browne pushed the car to a small town; there, closer to the reservation, he borrowed two gallons of gas from a station manager and hurried to the hospital at White Earth.

Wolfie Wight, the reservation doctor, an enormous woman, opened the hatchback; her wide head, hard grin, and cold hands menaced the child. "Almost brown," the doctor shouted. Later, she printed that name on the reservation birth certificate, with a flourish.

Almost was concerned with creations; his untraditional birth and perinatal name would explain, to some, his brute dedication to trickster simulations. No one, not even his parents, could re-member much about his childhood. He was alone, but not lonesome, a dreamer who traveled in trickster stories. He learned to read in back seats and matured in seven abandoned cars, his sanctuaries and private mansions on the reservation. Station wagons were his beds, closets, hospitals, libraries; and in other cars he conversed with mongrels, counted his contradictions, and overturned what he heard from the elders. He lived in the ruins of civilization and shouted at trees, screamed into panic holes; he was, in his own words, "a natural polyvinyl chloride partisan."

Almost started a new tribal world with the creation of a winter woman, an icewoman as enormous as the reservation doctor; she saluted and laughed at men. Hundreds of people drove from the cities and other reservations to hear the icewoman laugh, to watch her move her arms. The sound of her cold voice shivered into summer, into rash rumors that ran down the trickster. He was secure in the blood, a bold protester, an eminent romancer, but censure was a cold tribal hand.

Almost was never a failure in the tribal sense; he resisted institutions and honored chance but never conclusions or termination. His imagination overcame last words in education; he never missed a turn at machines, even those dead in the weeds.

Once, when he applied for work, he told the reservation president that he had earned a "chance doctorate" at the Manifest Destiny Graduate School in California. The president was impressed and hired the trickster as a tribal computer consultant. "Chance," he boasted later, was a "back seat degree." He wired the reservation with enough computer power to launch it into outer space.

Theories never interested the trickster, but he was a genius at new schemes and practices, and the mechanical transanimation of instincts. He saw memories and dreams as three dimensional, colors and motion, and used that to understand race and laser holograms. "Theories," he said, "come from institutions, from the scared and lonesome, from people who fear the realities of their parents." Theories, he said, were "rush hours."

Almost never said much; he worked on computers and held hands with a teacher at the government school. Em Wheeler lived in the woods with two gray mongrels; she was lonesome, thin at the shoulders, and she listened to tricksters. He told her that "creations were obvious, a rope burn, a boil on the nose, warm water, and much better than theories." He mussed theories and harnessed instincts, natural responses. For instance, the icewoman was animated by a caged mongrel wired to a solenoid, the source of electromotivation. When the mongrel moved, when his heartbeat leaped, the icewoman saluted. The wires, gears, and pulleys, hidden beneath chicken mesh and wire, were powered by solar batteries. "There you have it, sun, snow, and a cold sleight of hand," he mocked, "considerate winter moves." The mongrels barked, and the icewoman laughed and laughed at the visitors.

The trickster was an instinctive mechanician; communal sentiments and machines were his best teachers. He was a bear, a crow in a birch, a mongrel, and he reached in imagination to a postbiological world. Cold robotics and his communion with bears caused the same suspicious solicitude on the reservation. He practiced seven bear poses under a whole moon. Much later, when he was on trial in tribal court, he said he was a shaman, a bear shaman selenographer. "Tricksters have the bear power to enchant women with the moon." He persuaded seven women, three tribal and four white, to bare their bottoms to the moon each month.

The icewoman, snow machines that saluted, bears, and moon studies, however, were not cited as the main reasons for his banishment late that summer. He was responsible for those postshamanic laser holotropes that hovered over the reservation; lucent presidents from old peace medals and other figures danced, transformed the lakes and meadows, and terrified tribal families.

Almost was tried and removed to the cities because he studied electromagnetism, luminescence, and spectral memories; more than that, he deconstructed biological time and paraded western explorers in laser holograms. The pale figures loomed over the mission pond and blemished the clear summer nights on the reservation.

The Quidnunc Council, dominated by several mixed femagogues, gathered to consider the grimmest gossip about the trickster and his laser holotropes: the ghosts of white men returned to steal tribal land, harvest wild rice, and net fish. Sixgun, a detached stump puller, said he saw a white monster sprout six heads and suck up the lake six times. "Sucker Lake is down six feet from last year."

The best stories on the reservation would contain some technologies, the electromagnetic visuals of the trickster mechanism. The femagogues, in the end, told the tribal court to settle for the terror he had caused on the reservation with his laser holograms. The court convened in the preschool classroom; the trickster, the judge, other court officials, and witnesses were perched on little chairs.

"Almost, some say you are a wicked shaman, not with us the whole time," said the tribal judge. He leaned back on the little chair. His stomach rolled over his belt. His feet were wide. His thumbs were stained and churned when he listened. "Your dad and me go back a long time, we hunted together, so what is this business about six white heads sucking off a lake?"

"Lasers, nothing more," said Almost.

"Who are they?"

"Nobody," he said. "Laser light shows."

"Whose lights?"

"Laser holotropes."

"Indian?" asked the judge. "Where's he from then?"

"Nowhere, laser is a light."

"Laser, what's his last name again?"

"Holotropes, but that's not a real name."

"Does he shine on our reservation?"

"Laser is an image."

"Not when he shines our deer," said the judge.

"Listen," said the trickster. "Let me show you." Almost drew some pictures on a chalkboard and talked about reflections, northern lights, and natural luminescence, but not enough to understand laser holotropes. His mother told him that a real healer, a trickster with a vision, "must hold back some secrets." The tribal court, wise elders but not healers, would not believe a chalk and talk show in a preschool classroom. The tribal judge ordered the crossblood to demonstrate his laser holotropes that night over the mission pond at White Earth.

The court order reached tribal communities more than a hundred miles from the reservation. The loons wailed at the tribunal on the pond; mosquitoes whined in the moist weeds; fireflies traced the wide shore; bats wheeled and turned over the black water.

Christopher Columbus arose from the white pine, he saluted with a flourish, turned his head, circled the pond once, twice, three times, and then posed on the water tower. The school windows shimmered, blue and green light swarmed the building. Then, bright scuds carried the explorer to the center of the pond; there, his parts—an arm, hands, his loose head—protruded from the lucent scuds. Tribal families, the casual juries that night, gathered on the shore and cheered the dismemberment; later, when the explorer was put back together again and walked on water, most families retreated to the woods. One femagogue shouted that she could smell white diseases, the crotch of Christopher Columbus.

Almost Browne never revealed how he created the postshamanic laser holograms over the mission pond, but he told the tribal court that white men and diseases were not the same as electroluminations. "Columbus was here on a laser and withered with a wave of my hand," he said. "Laser holograms created the white man, but we set the memories and the skin colors."

"Not on your life," said a crossblood.

"Darker on the inside," the trickster countered.

"Never," she shouted.

"The laser is the new trickster."

"Not on this reservation, not a chance," said the tribal judge. Almost was held accountable for accidents, diseases, and death on the reservation that summer. He was shamed as a shaman and ordered to remove his machines and laser demons from the reservation; he was the first tribal member to be removed to the cities, a wild reversal of colonial histories. The trickster moved no one but the preschool teacher who held his hand and nurtured his imagination.

Em Wheeler had lived on the reservation for nineteen years, nine months, seventeen nights. She counted lonesome nights, and she held a calendar of contradictions and denials. The trial was held in her classroom; she listened, turned morose, and threatened to leave the reservation if the crossblood was removed.

Em and Almost lived in a camper van with two mongrels and a songbird in a bamboo cage. She smiled behind the wheel, liberated by a light show; he laughed, ate corn chips, and read newspaper stories out loud about their trickster laser shows. He was a natural at interviews. "Name the cities and we'll be there before winter," he told a television reporter. "We're on laser relocation." The reporter nodded and told him to repeat what he had said for a sound check. "Back on the reservation we presented holograms, white men over ponds and meadows," the trickster continued, "but in the cities we launched wild animals, tribal warriors, and presidents over the interstates."

"Will lasers replace traditions?"

"We need three lasers to create our light bears out there," he told the reporter, "so we bought two junkers with sun roofs and parked them in strategic places."

"How does it work?"

"Which one?"

"The bear over the interstate."

"Can't tell you," said the trickster.

"How about the presidents?"

"Peace medals."

"Show me your best president," she said to the camera.

"The nudes?"

"The police said your presidents are obscene."

"Light is no erection."

"Show me," the reporter teased.

"Lasers undress the peace presidents."

"Show me," she insisted.

"Lasers substantiate memories, dreams, with no obverse, no other, no shadows," he said. The trickster turned to the camera and pounced at the words; then he moved his mouth, saying in silence, "Lasers are the real world."

Hologramic warriors and wild animals over urban ponds were natural amusements, but when the trickster chased a bear and three moose over a rise on the interstate, no one on the road was pleased. Late traffic was slowed down for several miles; the bear was too close to the dividers and scared hundreds of drivers. Later, several people were interviewed on television and complained about the wild animals.

"That's why we spent billions for interstates," said a retired fireman, "to keep wild animals where they belong, in the woods, and out of harm's way in traffic."

"But the animals are light shows," said an interviewer.

"Right, but this guy ought to keep his lights to himself, his creation is not for me on the road," said the fireman. "Indians should know that much by now."

Almost and Em stopped traffic in several cities between Minneapolis and Detroit. The laser tricksters were cursed on the interstates, but he was celebrated on television talk shows and late night radio. Instant referenda revealed that native tribal people had natural rights to create animals over the cities; these rights, one woman insisted, were part of the treaties.

"These people have suffered enough," said a librarian, a caller on late night radio. "We took their land and resources; the least we can do now is be amused with their little light shows and metamorphoses."

"We watched in bed through our skylight," said another night talker. "Wild men, wild neighborhoods in the sky, me on my back, the tribes above, the whole thing is turned around somehow."

"We drove into the wilderness," a man whispered.

"Next thing you know we'll need a hunting license to drive home from work at night," said a woman on a television talk show. She was a trucker who drove cattle to market.

The trickster and the schoolteacher were precious minutes from arrest in most cities. At last, the two were located by the military, a special surveillance plane used to track drug smugglers, and cornered on a dead end road at a construction site in downtown Milwaukee.

The police impounded their lasers and ordered them to appear in court later that week. They were charged with causing a public disturbance, endangerment on an interstate, and amusements without a license.

Editorial columnists and media interviewers defended their tribal rights to the air, where there were no legal differences between light and sound. "Indians show, we sound; our rights are the same," a constitutional lawyer said on public radio.

The prosecutor, however, argued in court that the "two laser shiners" should be tried "because a light show is neither speech nor art, and is not protected by current copyright laws."

"The prosecutor is a racist," said a student.

"The creator in this case is a digital code, not a tribal artist," said the prominent prosecutor. "Furthermore, bright lights like loud music are a public nuisance and put basic transportation at risk."

Almost and Em represented themselves at the hearing. "Your honor, my chest is white but my heart is tribal," she said. The judge, on loan from a northern rural district, smiled, and others laughed in the crowded courtroom. "Remember when you were a child, silhouettes on the bedroom wall at night?"

"Make your point," said the judge.

"Well, lasers heal in three dimensions, a real silhouette, and besides, an animal of the light has a natural tribal right to the night, more so than a trucker with higher beams," said Em.

"You have a point there."

"Your honor, our presentation is procedural," pleaded the prosecutor. "This is not the proper forum for a lecture on candlepower." He pinched his chin, a measure of his pleasure over his last phrase. "We are prepared for trial."

"Christopher Columbus," shouted the trickster.

"Your witness?"

"Would you hold the right to his image over the road?" Almost pounded his chest several times, a filmic gesture, and then posed at the prow of the polished bench. "Columbus is our precedence."

"New World indeed, but the issue here is an interstate, not a novel port for the Niña, Pinta, Santa Maria," the prosecutor lectured. "Real bears and laser simulations have no legal voice in our courts, your honor. Their beams are not protected, not even in tribal courts."

"Then cut the lights."

"What?"

"Plead in the dark," said the trickster.

"Your honor, please. . . ."

"Then we have a right to be tried with our light."

"Your honor, please, the accused was removed from the reservation for the same cause, the perilous light that comes before this court," said the prosecutor. "Their new cause is not sacred but postbiological as we read Hans Moravec in *Mind Children*, and this world 'will host a great range of individuals constituted from libraries of accumulated knowledge.'"

"Can the lard," said the judge.

"Christopher Columbus is all over the place," the trickster continued, "in lights, kites, trailers on planes, but his image is no more important than a warrior, a bear over the road at night."

"What is the cause here?"

"Light, light," lauded the trickster, "is a tribal right."

"First Amendment lights?"

"First and Sixth," shouted Em, "lights and rights."

"Due process?"

"Feral lasers," said the trickster, and then the lights were turned out. Lucent animals, superconductors on the dark, appeared as defendants. Then the spectators chanted two words, feral laser, feral laser, faster and faster. The trickster lasers created a wild Mount Rushmore National Memorial. George Washington, Jefferson, Lincoln, and Theodore Roosevelt beamed over the bench; however, tribal warriors eclipsed the presidents in a new tribunal.

Meanwhile, in old and troubled cities across the nation, people by the thousands bought lasers to revise histories, to hold their memories, and to create a new wilderness over the interstates. The cities came alive with laser holograms, a communal light show, a right to come together in the night. Lights danced over the cities; lonesome figures returned to their lost houses.

"The laser is a tribal pen, a light brush in the wild air," the judge pronounced, overcome with light amusement, "and these warriors are new creations, an interior landscape, memories to be sure, an instance of communal rights and free expression." The judge ruled in favor of light rights and dismissed the case; he appeared that night with the animals over seven cities.

Antoine de la Mothe Cadillac, tribal mummers in the new fur trade, peace medal presidents, bears, and crows appeared with Almost Browne and Em Wheeler in a comic opera, trickster lasers on a summer night over the Renaissance Center in Detroit.

Ice Tricksters

UNCLE CLEMENT told me last night that he knows *almost* everything. Almost, that's his nickname and favorite word in stories, lives with me and my mother in a narrow house on the Leech Lake Chippewa Indian Reservation in northern Minnesota.

Last night, just before dark, we drove into town to meet my cousin at the bus depot and to buy rainbow ice cream in thick brown cones. Almost sat in the back seat of our old car and started his stories the minute we were on the dirt road around the north side of the lake on our way to town. The wheels bounced and raised thick clouds of dust and the car doors shuddered. He told me about the time he almost started an ice cream store when he came back from the army. My mother laughed and turned to the side. The car rattled on the washboard road. She shouted, "I heard that one before!"

"Almost!" he shouted back.

"What almost happened?" I asked. My voice bounced with the car.

"Well, it was winter then," he said. Fine brown dust settled on his head and the shoulders of his overcoat. "Too cold for ice cream in the woods, but the idea came to mind in the summer, almost."

"Almost, you know almost everything about nothing," my mother shouted and then laughed, "or almost nothing about almost everything."

"Pincher, we're almost to the ice cream," he said and brushed me on the head with his right hand. He did that to ignore what my mother said about what he knows. Clouds of dust covered the trees behind us on both sides of the road.

Almost is my great-uncle, and he decides on our nicknames, even the nicknames for my cousins who live in the cities and visit the reservation in the summer. Pincher, the name he gave me, was natural because I pinched my way through childhood. I learned about the world between two fingers. I pinched everything, or *almost* everything, as my uncle would say. I pinched animals, insects, leaves, water, fish, ice cream, the moist air, winter breath, snow, and even words, the words I could see or almost see. I pinched the words and learned how to speak sooner than my cousins. Pinched words are easier to remember. Some words, like government and grammar, are unnatural, never seen and never pinched. Who could pinch a word like grammar?

Almost named me last winter when my grandmother was sick with pneumonia and died on the way to the public health hospital. She had no teeth and covered her mouth when she smiled, almost a child. I sat in the back seat of the car and held her thin brown hand. Even her veins were hidden, it was so cold that night. On the road we pinched summer words over the hard snow and ice. She smiled and said, *papakine, papakine,* over and over. That means cricket or grasshopper in our tribal language and we pinched that word together. We pinched *papakine* in the back seat of our cold car on the way to the hospital. Later she whispered *bisanagami sibi,* the river is still, and then she died. My mother straightened her fingers, but later, at the wake in our house, my grandmother pinched a summer word and we could see that. She was buried in the cold earth with a warm word between her fingers. That's when my uncle gave me my nickname.

Almost never told lies, but he used the word almost to stretch the truth like a tribal trickster, my mother told me. The trickster is a character in stories, an animal, or person, even a tree at times, who pretends the world can be stopped with words, and he frees the world in stories. Almost said the trickster is almost a man and almost a woman, and almost a child, a clown who laughs and plays games with words in stories. The trickster is almost a free spirit. Almost told me about the trickster many times, and I think I almost understand his stories. He brushed my head with his hand and said, "The almost world is a better world, a sweeter dream than the world we are taught to understand in school."

"I understand, almost," I told my uncle.

"People are almost stories, and stories tell almost the whole truth," Almost told me last winter when he gave me my nickname. "Pincher is your nickname and names are stories too, *gega*." The word *gega* means *almost* in the Anishinaabe or Chippewa language.

"Pincher *gega*," I said and then tried to pinch a tribal word I could not yet see clear enough to hold between my fingers. I could almost see *gega*.

Almost, no matter the season, wore a long overcoat. He bounced when he walked, and the thick bottom of the overcoat hit the ground. The sleeves were too short but he never minded that because he could eat and deal cards with no problems. So there he was in line for a rainbow ice cream cone, dressed for winter, or almost winter he would say. My mother wonders if he wears that overcoat for the attention.

"*Gega, gega,*" an old woman called from the end of the line.

"You spending some claims money on ice cream or a new coat?" No one ignored his overcoat.

"What's that?" answered Almost. He cupped his ear to listen because he knew the old woman wanted to move closer, ahead in the line. The claims money she mentioned is a measure of everything on the reservation. The federal government promised to settle a treaty over land with tribal people. Almost and thousands of others have been waiting for more than a century to be paid for land that was taken from them. There were rumors at least once a week that federal checks were in the mail, final payment for the broken treaties. When white people talk about a rain dance, tribal people remember the claims dancers who promised a federal check in every mailbox.

"Claims money," she whispered in the front of the line.

"Almost got a check this week," Almost said and smiled.

"Almost is as good as nothing," she said back.

"Pincher gets a bicycle when the claims money comes."

"My husband died waiting for the claims settlement," my mother said. She looked at me and then turned toward the ice cream counter to order. I held back my excitement about a new bicycle because the claims money might never come; no one was ever sure. Almost believed in rumors, and he waited one morning for a check to appear in his mailbox on the reservation. Finally, my mother scolded him for wasting his time on promises made by the government. "You grow old too fast on government promises," she said. "Anyway, the government has nothing to do with bicycles." He smiled at me and we ate our rainbow ice cream cones at the bus depot. That was a joke because the depot is nothing more than a park bench in front of a restaurant. On the back of the bench was a sign that announced an ice sculpture contest to be held in the town park on July Fourth.

"Ice cube sculpture?" asked my mother.

"No blocks big enough around here in summer," I said, thinking about the ice sold to tourists, cubes and small blocks for camp coolers.

"Pig Foot, he cuts ice from the lake in winter and stores it in a cave, buried in straw," my uncle whispered. He looked around, concerned that someone might hear about the ice cave. "Secret *mikwam*, huge blocks, enough for a great sculpture." The word *mikwam* means ice.

"Never mind," my mother said as she licked the ice cream on her fingers. The rainbow turned pink when it melted. The pink ran over her hand and under her rings.

Black Ice was late, but that never bothered her because she liked to ride in the back of buses at night. She sat in the dark and pretended that she could see the people who lived under the distant lights. She lived in a dark apartment building in Saint Paul with her mother and older brother and made the world come alive with light more than with sound or taste. She was on the reservation for more than a month last summer, and we thought her nickname would be Light or Candle or something like that, even though she wore black clothes. Not so. Almost avoided one obvious name and chose another when she attended our grandmother's funeral. Black Ice had never been on the reservation in winter. She slipped and fell seven times on black ice near the church and so she got that as a nickname.

Black Ice was the last person to leave the bus. She held back behind the darkened windows as long as she could. Yes, she was shy, worried about being embarrassed in public. I might be that way too, if we lived in an apartment in the cities, but the only public on the reservation are the summer tourists. She was happier when we bought her a rainbow ice cream cone. She was dressed in black, black everything, even black canvas shoes, no, almost black. The latest television style in the cities. Little did my uncle know that her reservation nickname would describe a modern style of clothes. We sat in the back seat on the way back to our house. We could smell the dust in the dark, in the tunnel of light through the trees. The moon was new that night.

"Almost said he would buy me my first bicycle when he gets his claims money," I told Black Ice. She brushed her clothes; there was too much dust.

"I should've brought my new mountain bike," she said. "I don't use it much though. Too much traffic and you have to worry about it being stolen."

"Should we go canoeing? We have a canoe."

"Did you get television yet?" asked Black Ice.

"Yes," I boasted, "my mother won a big screen with a dish and everything at a bingo game on the reservation." We never watched much television though.

"Really?"

"Yes, we can get more than a hundred channels."

"On the reservation?"

"Yes, and bingo too."

"Well, here we are, paradise at the end of a dust cloud," my mother announced as she turned down the trail to our house on the lake. The headlights held the eyes of a raccoon, and we could smell a skunk in the distance. Low branches brushed the side of the car; we were home. We sat in the car for a few minutes and listened to the night. The dogs were panting. Mosquitoes, so big we called them the state bird, landed on our arms, bare knuckles, and warm shoulder blades. The water was calm and seemed to hold back a secret dark blue light from the bottom of the lake. One loon called and another answered. One thin wave rippled over the stones on the shore. We ducked mosquitoes and went into the house. We were tired, and too tired in the morning to appreciate the plan to carve a trickster from a block of ice.

Pig Foot lived alone on an island. He came down to the wooden dock to meet us in the morning. We were out on the lake before dawn, my uncle at the back of the canoe in his over- coat. We paddled and he steered us around the point of the is- land where bald eagles nested.

"Pig Foot?" questioned Black Ice.

"Almost gave him that nickname," I whispered to my cousin as we came closer to the dock. "Watch his little feet; he prances like a pig when he talks. The people in town swear his feet are hard and cloven."

"Are they?"

"No," I whispered as the canoe touched the dock.

"Almost," shouted Pig Foot.

"Almost," said Almost. "Pincher, you know him from the funeral, and this lady is from the city. We named her Black Ice."

"*Makate Mikwam*," said Pig Foot. "Black ice comes with the white man and roads. No black ice on this island." He tied the canoe to the dock and patted his thighs with his open hands. The words *makate mikwam* mean black ice.

Black Ice looked down at Pig Foot's feet when she stepped out of the canoe. He wore black overshoes, the toes were turned out. She watched him prance on the rough wooden dock when he talked about the weather and mosquitoes. The black flies and mosquitoes on the island, special breeds, were more vicious than anywhere else on the reservation. Pig Foot was pleased that no one camped on the island because of the black flies. Some people accused him of raising mean flies to keep the tourists away. "Not a bad idea, now that I think about it," said Pig Foot. He had a small bunch of black hair on his chin. He pulled the hair when he was nervous and revealed a row of short stained teeth. Black Ice turned toward the sunrise and held her laughter.

"We come to see the ice cave," said Almost. "We need a large block to win the ice sculpture contest in four days."

"What ice cave is that?" asked Pig Foot.

"The almost secret one!" shouted Almost.

"That one, sure enough," said Pig Foot. He mocked my uncle and touched the lapel of his overcoat. "I was wondering about that contest. What does ice have to do with July Fourth?" He walked ahead as he talked, and then every eight steps he would stop and turn to wait for us. But if you were too close you would bump into him when he stopped. Black Ice counted his steps, and when we were near the entrance to the ice cave she imitated his prance, toes turned outward. She pranced seven steps and then waited for him to turn on the eighth.

Pig Foot stopped in silence on the shore where the bank was higher and where several trees leaned over the water. There, in the vines and boulders, we could feel the cool air. A cool breath on the shore.

Pig Foot told us we could never reveal the location of the ice cave, but he said we could tell stories about ice and the great spirit of winter in summer. He said this because most tribal stories should be told in winter, not in summer when evil spirits could be about to listen and do harm to words and names. We agreed to the conditions and followed him over the boulders into the wide cold cave. We could hear our breath, even a heartbeat. Whispers were too loud in the cave.

"Almost the scent of winter on July Fourth," whispered Almost. "In winter we overturn the ice in shallow creeks to smell the rich blue earth, and then in summer we taste the winter in this ice cave, almost."

"Almost, you're a poet, sure enough, but that's straw, not

the smell of winter," said Pig Foot. He was hunched over where
the cave narrowed at the back. Beneath the mounds of straw
were huge blocks of ice, lake ice, blue and silent in the cave. Was
that thunder, or the crack of winter ice on the lake? "Just me,
dropped a block over the side." In winter he sawed blocks of ice
in the bay where it was the thickest and towed the blocks into
the cave on an aluminum slide. Pig Foot used the ice to cool his
cabin in summer, but Almost warned us that there were other
reasons. Pig Foot believes that the world is becoming colder and
colder, the ice thicker and thicker. Too much summer in the
blood would weaken him, so he rests on a block of ice in the cave
several hours a week to stay in condition for the coming of the
ice age on the reservation.

"Black Ice, come over here," said Almost. "Stretch out on
this block." My cousin brushed the straw from the ice and leaned
back on the block. "Almost, almost, now try this one, no this
one, almost."

"Almost what?" asked Black Ice.

"Almost a whole trickster," whispered Almost. Then he told
us what he had in mind. A trickster, he wanted us to carve a
tribal trickster to enter in the ice sculpture contest.

"What does a trickster look like?" I asked. Trickster was a
word I could not see, there was nothing to pinch. How could I
know a trickster between my fingers?

"Almost like a person," he said and brushed the straw from
a block as large as me. "Almost in there, we have three days to
find the trickster in the ice."

Early the next morning we paddled across the lake to the ice
cave to begin our work on the ice trickster. We were dressed for
winter. I don't think my mother believed us when we told her
about the ice cave. "Almost," she said with a smile, "finally
found the right place to wear his overcoat in the summer."

Pig Foot was perched on a block of ice when we arrived. We

slid the block that held the trickster to the center of the cave and set to work with an ax and chisels. We rounded out a huge head, moved down the shoulders, and on the second day we freed the nose, ears, and hands of the trickster. I could see him in the dark blue ice; the trickster was almost free. I could almost pinch the word trickster.

Almost directed as we carved the ice on the first and second days, but on the third and final day he surprised us. We were in the cave dressed in winter coats and hats, ready to work, when he told us to make the final touches on our own, to liberate the face of the trickster. Almost and Pig Foot leaned back on a block of ice; we were in charge of who the trickster would become in ice.

Black Ice wanted the trickster to look like a woman. I wanted the ice sculpture to look like a man. The trickster, we decided, would be both, one side a man and the other side a woman. The true trickster, almost a man and almost a woman. In the end the ice trickster had features that looked like our uncle, our grandmother, and other members of our families. The trickster had small feet turned outward, he wore an overcoat, and she pinched her fingers on one hand. He was ready for the contest, she was the ice trickster on July Fourth.

That night we tied sheets around the ice trickster and towed her behind the canoe to the park on the other side of the lake. The ice floated and the trickster melted slower in the water. We rounded the south end of the island and headed to the park near the town, slow and measured like traders on a distant sea. The park lights reflected on the calm water. We tied the ice trickster to the end of the town dock and beached our canoe. We were very excited, but soon we were tired and slept on the grass in the park near the dock. The trickster was a liberator; she would win on Independence Day. Almost, anyway.

"The trickster melted," shouted Almost. He stood on the

end of the dock, a sad uncle in his overcoat, holding the rope and empty sheets. At first we thought he had tricked us, we thought the whole thing was a joke, so we laughed. We rolled around on the grass and laughed. Almost was not amused at first. He turned toward the lake to hide his face, but then he broke into wild laughter. He laughed so hard he almost lost his balance in that heavy overcoat. He almost fell into the lake.

"The ice trickster won at last," said Black Ice.

"No, wait, she almost won. No ice trickster would melt that fast in the lake," he said and ordered us to launch the canoe for a search. Overnight the trickster had slipped from the sheets and floated free from the dock, somewhere out in the lake. The ice trickster was free on July Fourth.

We paddled the canoe in circles and searched for hours and hours but we could not find the ice trickster. Later, my mother rented a motorboat and we searched in two circles.

Almost was worried that the registration would close, so he abandoned the search and appealed to the people who organized the ice sculpture competition. They agreed to extend the time, and they even invited other contestants to search for the ice trickster. The lake was crowded with motorboats.

"There she floats," a woman shouted from a fishing boat. We paddled out and towed the trickster back to the dock. Then we hauled her up the bank to the park and a pedestal. We circled the pedestal and admired the ice trickster.

"Almost a trickster," said Almost. We looked over the other entries. There were more birds than animals, more heads than hips or hands, and the other ice sculptures were much smaller. Dwarfs next to the ice trickster. She had melted some overnight in the lake, but he was still head and shoulders above the other entries. The competition was about to close when we learned that there was a height restriction. Almost never read the rules. No entries over three feet and six inches in any direction. The other entries were much smaller. No one found large blocks of ice in town, so they were all within the restrictions. Our trickster was four feet tall, or at least she was that tall when we started out in the ice cave.

"No trickster that started out almost he or she can be too much of either," said Almost. We nodded in agreement, but we were not certain what he meant.

"What now?" asked Black Ice.

"Get a saw," my mother ordered. "We can cut that trickster down a notch or two on the bottom." She held her hand about four inches from the base to see what a shorter trickster would look like.

"Almost short enough," said Almost. "He melted some, she needs to lose four more inches by my calculations. We should have left her in the lake for another hour."

Pig Foot turned the trickster on his side, but when we measured four inches from the bottom he protested. "Not the feet, not my feet, those are my feet on the trickster."

"Not my ear either."

"Not the hands," I pleaded.

"The shins," shouted Black Ice. No one had claimed the shins on the ice trickster, so we measured and sawed four inches from his shins and then carved the knees to fit the little pig feet.

"Almost whole," announced Almost.

"What's a trickster?" asked the three judges who hurried down the line of pedestals before the ice sculptures melted beyond recognition.

"Almost a person," said Black Ice.

"What person?"

"My grandmother," I told the judges. "See how she pinched her fingers. She was a trickster; she pinched a cricket there." Pig Foot was nervous; he pranced around the pedestal.

The judges prowled back and forth, whispered here and

there between two pedestals, and then they decided that there would be two winners because they could not decide on one. "The winners are the Boy and His Dog, and that ice trickster, Almost a Person," the judges announced.

The ice trickster won a bicycle, a large camp cooler, a dictionary, and twelve double rainbow cones. The other ice cave sculptors gave me the bicycle because I had never owned one before, and because the claims payment might be a bad promise. We divided the cones as best we could between five people, Almost, Pig Foot, Black Ice, me, and my mother.

Later, we packed what remained of the ice trickster, including the shin part, and took him back to the ice cave, where she lasted for more than a year. She stood in the back of the cave without straw and melted down to the last drop of a trickster. She was almost a whole trickster, almost.

The Red Coin

CALENDARS and clocks hold her best seasons; crows in the winter birch, moths at the window, striders on water are separated in her memories. She avers and pretends that stories and the souvenirs that haunt her head are contained, anchored to the clock.

Yet when the material cues are unbuttoned, the past runs wild in her presence. Last week she presented a rare red coin at a conference on new insurance policies, and we heard a rush of trade stories about hard winters more than a century ago on Madeline Island in Lake Superior.

Bunnie La Pointe, reservation born and wearied, lost the anchor in the cities; now she is aroused by seven alarm clocks, one for each month that she has been on board in the health policies division at the Marshall Moon Insurance Companies of Milwaukee, Wisconsin.

She completed a secretarial course, third in a class of nineteen, at a rural vocational school near the reservation; one week later she moved downtown to live with her sister in a condominium. "She packed lock, stock, and tomorrow," said her best uncle, Crack La Pointe, "for a mortar landscape that holds bad time on a broken leash." The seven clocks are an unusual accommodation to the cold concrete near Lake Michigan.

Bunnie, a tribal nickname that praised her sericeous thighs, wide and brown, was tormented by men on the reservation. She complained that tribal men were as "odious as mongrels, minimal machines of the night, and then some," she reminded her sister Brave. She loathed their odors and noises, what men do to women, chairs, beds, bathrooms, "what night and drink do to their breath and manners."

This hatred, she told her best uncle, was absolved with an urban career, separation from the reservation; but now, lonesome in a high-rise condominium, she hears the same tribal men in clocks, on the tick of time. She cowers when someone cites the hour, covers her ears, but she would never stop clocks or turn down the moment.

"Time hates me here," she printed on a picture postcard to her mother, who lives on the White Earth Reservation. "Strangers stop me to ask the time, clocks scream at me, torment me, haunt me, and that terrible ticktock reminds me of the men back there, even the sound of the time clock at work bothers me." The postman read the message out loud on his route and twice more at the Little Red Wagon. The customers snickered, and the owner of the reservation tavern and general store wound his stock of clocks and set the alarms to celebrate, on the hour, her nocturnal misfortunes downtown.

Bunnie covered her head with the pillow. Eight alarms sounded at dawn beside her bed; the luminous dials became the faces of tribal men, the ticktocks their harsh noises. "Once there was a woman who turned cold and white in the concrete," said one clock, ticktock. "Come swim with me, the water is warm," said another clock face.

"No more time," she screamed at the clocks; even so, she

counted the slow minutes that morning as she drove at high speed from the underground garage, through more than seven stop lights, turned twice too close to the pedestrians, and reached the shore of Lake Michigan. She rumbled over the curb, parked at an angle on the sidewalk.

There, she screamed once more, unbuckled her narrow shoes and double dial watch, threw them into the back seat with the red coin, and tumbled down the bank to a sandstone cave where she hid from the clocks, the past, and her memories. No ticktocks sounded over the cold high waves.

The minimal measures of men and corporate hours, old television schedules, consumed seasons, material kismet, had echoed with esteem in her memories, in her new career and practiced signatures. She praised insurance and proposed tribal health policies as "our new healers on the reservations." The postman read that much at the tavern; there were wild cures at hand that night.

Crack had his reasons to remember these stories. The clock panic and other problems had started last month when his niece lost her "heart station" on her first visit to Madeline Island, the largest of the Apostle Islands in Lake Superior. Heart stations, he said, were natural moments, "a brush with pure creation, unclocked, the third hand on the hour." Since then, time had been her tormentor; the clocks hold wicked men and ticktocks their trickeries. She covered time on the later moves; her dreams were wild, mottled with men and disconnected scenes from past generations.

Bunnie toured the lagoon and studied historical documents in the museum on the island. Later, at dusk, she waded in the clear warm water and then rested on the beach near ancient tribal communities. There, when she pressed a castle into the white sand, the coin appeared, blood colored. She washed the thin spe-

cie and polished it on her sleeve; in the late light she discovered
her last name was struck on both sides of the coin. She was alone
and bewildered. Worried that the coin was the sign of a wicked
shaman, she ran to the home of the museum curator. He explained that several fur traders printed their names on coins;
however, he could not account for the rich red color. The coin
was not copper, but no one on the island could name the metal.

Wild histories abound in her dreams now; the second ticktock on a common clock cleaves remembrance, conversations,
rumors at the tavern; stories run loose from her minor tribal past.
The steam baths, tennis courts, chrome and foam furniture in
the condominium buried, for eight months, her woodland memories. Her parents remain on the reservation in a narrow house
with a woodstove and several mongrels. The red coin overturned
the moment; the tribal past crashed on the clocks.

Crack La Pointe told his niece, "Carve on a birch stick the
worst times you can remember, mark your bad memories, and
then burn it, one notch at a time. That's the best cure for clock
panic." She listened to the old man, but she was never at ease
with his mongrels. Crack moves words into the present with his
hands, teases time into the oral tradition; he stammers at verbs
but he never backslides. The interior landscapes in his stories are
wind driven; the meadows rebound and the past withers the
hours on the clock.

Bunnie listened and listened, but she could never repeat his
stories. Her meadows were material, a landscape with no shadows, a supermarket remembrance. Her income was high enough
to leave the reservation, high enough to purchase a convertible,
designer clothes. She was content in a high-rise with a view of
cars and airplanes. She told the mirrors that she was real in a
condominium, real until that red coin appeared on the island.

Bunnie never cared much about reservation histories, and

she told her sister that she never wanted to be a tribal person in the first place. "Indians are sentenced to reservations," she asserted. "What sort of histories are we to remember?"

"Search me," said Brave.

"Do people make histories out of prison sentences?"

"No way," said Brave.

"Who wants to look like a cracked picture?"

"No one," said Brave.

"Who would be an old brown photograph?"

"No one," repeated Brave.

"Anthropologists, that's who made us brown," said Bunnie.

"Right," said Brave.

"No, no, not me."

"Not me either," said Brave.

"Boreman buried that red coin," said Bunnie.

"Tribal clocks, ticktock, beat their time, ticktock in the old pine," Crack said to High Boreman, the cultural anthropologist who fancied tribal women, especially the La Pointe sisters, and who had organized the search for Bunnie. The anthropologist touched his enormous black wristwatch when he listened; a peculiar person who signs his name to ideas and theories. He lectures on fur trade cultures, studies shamanism, and collects rare coins.

Crack teased, "Boreman reads the hours on our hands, his clocks are coins, ticktock, ticktock. Too bad he cuts his time with plastic flowers, dead calendars on the white side."

"Where is the red coin?" asked Boreman.

"Bunnie has it," said Crack.

"So, the search begins."

"Not until Tune Browne gets back," said Crack.

"White Earth Tune?"

"None other."

"Why Tune?" asked Boreman.

"He's got the best mongrels," said Crack.

"That's an oxymoron."

"Right, a reservation's an oxymoron, pure mongrels, tribal dances on the Fourth of July, how about that," said Crack. "Bunnie learned them from me, and she won the annual White Earth Oxymora Competition twice in a row with 'warm winter' and 'treaty rights,' but 'white blood' and 'indian time' are her best ones."

Bunnie moved closer to the mirror to hold her breath. Last week was too wild. She heard stories about the hard winters on the island. At first she tried to resist the reckless voices, but the mirror brought her closer to the woodstove in the American Fur Company Store on Madeline Island. Several men were boasting, as usual, about old times, adventures, the storms, the cold, women, and near disasters on Lake Superior. The fur trade was not the same; in the old days there were more animals. The markets were weakened by territorial politics, competition, and new fashions. "Never too worried," said a trader, a crossblood with a brown moustache, "hundred and nine barrels packed with fish, and corn, stored over the last season, enough to feed the whole island, even some visitors." Three old traders worried in their stories.

The provident missionaries on the island were never without burdens, the real and the demonic; starvation was on their minds. The pale mission women, withered behind thunder and lace and marooned on a celestial centerfold, chewed their cheeks inside over the stories practiced at the American Fur Company Store. The tricksters raised their brows to move a sentence, pinched their ears to widen the comedies that would swerve generations much later in mirrors and at conferences in the cold concrete.

Tune Browne, crossblood woodland shaman and founder of the New School of Socioacupuncture, a tribal muster of trickster remedies, antidotes, and exalted contradictions that release the ritual terror in pictures and captured images, popped his wide red parasol and called his two mongrels to his side, to his over-stuffed throne in a small downtown apartment cornered by asphalt parking lots. Pensive and White Lies, the mongrels, laughed at the trickster healer.

"Bunnie has vanished," said Crack.

"Where?" asked Tune. He wagged his hand and the mongrels circled the throne. Pensive was brown with three white paws; one front paw had been severed in a beaver trap. White Lies had white amoeboid blotches on her head and black sides.

"The Little Red Tavern, but she was downtown on the post-card. We heard the clocks and she never came back," said Crack. Pensive savored his socks and stained crotch and then sneezed.

"White Lies knows where to find our women downtown," said the trickster. He never seemed to believe his own pronouncements. "She can track a sweet crotch from a nickname to a cold hand in a high-rise, believe me," said Tune.

"Who?" asked Boreman.

"White Lies, of course," said Tune.

"Downtown?"

"Bring me a pair of panties."

"Wait a minute."

"Boreman, unbend; the panties are for the mongrels," said Crack.

"Human or otherwise?" asked Boreman.

"The panties, please."

"What pair?"

"The tight bikinis."

"What color?" asked Crack. He sorted the bright colors, blue and red, to the side and selected a cream pair with her name on the rear. "Put the mongrels on this brand."

"White Lies smells; she can't read yet," said Tune.

"Take your pick."

"These are clean. We need a stained crotch," said Tune.

"Mongrels in the clover," said Boreman. He touched the name on the cream with one hand and folded a blue bikini into his pocket. The mongrels laughed at the anthropologist.

White Lies was unhurried. She toured the condominium, mirror to mirror, and then sat down in the kitchen. Pensive raced to the bedrooms, nosed into corners, closets, and located a basket of soiled underclothes.

The mongrels laughed on the elevator down to the garage and raced out to the street. The searchers, an anthropologist and two crossblood tricksters, followed the mongrels through seven stop lights, paused at a meat market, and circled a park. The mongrels were soon out of sight, closer to Lake Michigan.

Pensive leaped into the convertible parked on the sidewalk and pushed his paws on the horn; the others heard the sound, a high-pitched unusual cadence. White Lies retrieved the shoes and wristwatch from the back seat. The mongrels licked the shoes, leather seats, and head rests.

Tune tied the panties and the expensive watch to the end of a long birch stick; he used clear fish line so the panties soared and the watch appeared to move in space. He threw the shoes over the bank. The wind was brisk on the lake. The clock panic cure was at hand.

The mongrels laughed and wagged down closer to the sand-stone cave; the anthropologist who fancied tribal women, and the tricksters who mocked women, were close behind, hand to tree down the steep bank to the lake.

Bunnie heard the waves break and rush back on the black stones, nothing more. She huddled at the back of the cave, chin on her knees, and waited for the waves to rise, to haul her back to the sea. She would become a stone, a smooth brown stone. "No clocks, no tribes, never reservations as a stone," she boasted. She would be a stone with geomantic bands on her head and hands from fires, floods, and glaciers.

White Lies smelled her in the earth, the press of her wide toes on the cold stones; she raised her wet nose, hesitated twice, and then leaned closer to the cave. Pensive laughed at the sensual pleasures of a human crotch and bounded across the stones to the entrance; he howled and rushed to the scent, a mongrel between her thighs. Bunnie saw a tribal man in the cold mist and bashed the mongrel with her bare feet. Pensive tumbled backward over the stones and into the water; a wave carried him to the shore. White Lies waited at the side of the cave.

Tune lowered the wristwatch and panties over the cave entrance; the panties billowed and the watch turned in the wind. The trickster moved the birch stick from side to side, teased the panties on the line. He was certain that she would respond to her best monogrammed underclothes.

Bunnie shivered, tormented and embarrassed; she threw stones and hit the watch three times. The scene was hurried, two crows spied the watch and caught the clear fish line instead. The watch dropped and the waves rolled it between the stones. The panties floated out of reach and settled on a bush above the cave.

Boreman was stimulated by the wind in the panties. He leaned too close to the edge, lost his balance, and slid on the stone. He held on to a small tree; his legs dangled over the entrance to the cave. The thin anthropologist wriggled on the tree.

His trousers loosened and the blue panties he had stolen came out of his pocket and spread open on the wet stones. Then he lost his grip and fell into the cave.

Bunnie cursed and rushed the anthropologist. She kicked him and then pounced on his narrow chest; she sat on his face and pressed her cold wet crotch over his mouth. He struggled to breathe.

"Creep," she shouted, "you stole my panties and planted that red coin in the sand." Bunnie could have smothered the anthropologist if her uncle had not interceded. Boreman rolled on his side and wiped his mouth with his sleeve; he was breathless and ecstatic.

"That voice is back," said Crack.

"The watch is dead, panties on the brush," said Tune. "Now we burn the birch stick and pass the red coin." The trickster started a fire at the back of the cave and the mongrels gathered closer. The waves rolled higher and splashed on the stones at the entrance.

"Crack, the past is loose," pleaded Bunnie.

"Burn the birch," said Tune.

"Scorch the bad memories," said Crack.

"Cut me a piece," she shouted. She threw a thin splinter of birch on the fire and cursed the anthropologist. "Boreman burns for the past and the bad memories he caused with that red coin." Crack cut more birch, and the more she cursed the more she burned, a liberation blaze. "Burn that wicked teacher at the government school on the reservation," she shouted. White Lies laughed and moved closer to her wide brown thighs. Pensive held his distance, cold, bruised, and wet. "Burn the clocks, burn the missionaries, burn those rude reservation men, burn bad memories, and burn those bad tricksters."

"Fireproof tricksters here," said Tune.

"Burn my watch," she ordered and threw another splinter on the fire. The flames leaped higher and the sandstone cave was alive with wild lights and shadows. "Cut more birch," she demanded. She burned teachers, lovers, wicked old men, and she tried to burn tribal tricksters. At last she burned the clocks and calendars, souvenirs that haunted her memories.

"Burn the red coin," said Bunnie.

"No, not here," said Crack.

"That coin must burn," she pleaded.

"No, the red coin must be deposited," said Tune.

"Where?"

"Somewhere downtown."

"When?"

"Now, to be precise," said Tune.

"Where is it?" asked Crack.

"Back seat of the car with my watch," said Bunnie.

"No time to waste," said Tune. He threw the last slivers of birch into the fire and waved the mongrels out with his hat. The anthropologist had vanished when his name was thrown into the fire. Bunnie and the tricksters climbed the bank back to the lake road. The mongrels leaped into the back seat and waited, side by side, for a ride in the convertible.

"That coin must be here," said Bunnie. She reached under the seats, searched the carpets. The mongrels laughed and watched her hands move between the seats. The leather was warm. At last, she touched the red coin behind the back seat.

"The coin, please," said Tune.

"Not so fast," said Bunnie.

"Give him the coin," said Crack.

"Tell me what for?"

"She's cured," sighed Crack.

"The past will haunt you unless we deposit the coin before dark," said Tune. His voice was serious, an unusual tone for a trickster. He waited at the side of the convertible with his hands in his pockets.

"But where?" asked Bunnie.

"Does it matter?'

"Yes, a bank, parking meter, video games, where?"

"A copy machine," said Tune.

"What?"

"Copy machines go wild on shaman coins."

"To be sure you're not just after the power of my coin, then let me make the deposit," she said. The tricksters and mongrels climbed into the convertible. Bunnie drove to the copy center at the university library.

"Perfect place to unload the past," said Tune.

"Shit, the coin is hot," said Bunnie. She opened her hand when they passed through the turnstile. The coin had marked her palm in two places, a red impression of her name in reverse. "What makes this thing so hot?"

The tricksters and mongrels, pursued by two librarians, circled a high speed copy machine. Tune muttered something about shamans, stones, and water, and then told Bunnie to deposit the coin. She hesitated, the coin was hot between her fingers and left a mark. She blinked twice and pushed the coin into the slot.

The machine was silent at first, and then a light flashed from under the cover, red lights beamed from seams in the machine. The machine hummed and copies shot out, faster and faster, random copies from copied memories, pages from the past covered the floor of the copy center. The librarians threw the master power switch, but the machine ran on the memories of past power. The mongrels laughed at the copies, red and white, thousands of copies.

Bunnie La Pointe was liberated from the clocks and tribal stories from the past. She returned to the condominium, cleaned the mirrors, and washed her monogrammed panties. Copies of the past endured in a machine with that rare red coin.

Pure Gumption

FATHER Father Mother is a trickster healer. Beneath his warm hands the bored and lonesome are mended and the sick are cured, but the church patriarchs were suspicious and banished the crossblood priest to a remote parish at Fortuna, North Dakota. There, on a cold winter night, he was invested as a potent member of the Flat Earth Society.

Double Father, as he was known on the baronage at the time he was ordained, was seldom surprised when cold reason blundered on ecclesiastical rails, because he was closer to the animals in a human than he was to the mind of a curial primate. He was the grandson of Novena Mae Ironmoccasin and Luster Browne, the Baron of Patronia. The trickster was born on the reservation, liberated on the prairie, and pleased to be a member of the Flat Earth Society with men and women who believed in the plain and evident.

The narrow chapel was perched at the high end of a gravel road two blocks north of a withered bank and one block east of a gun and antique dealer. The bank had failed fifty-four years ago in the same year that Gun and Content Hanson were married by the last pastor to serve their curious unincorporated town. That winter the old priest died in a wicked blizzard, and the chapel became the main base of the liberal council of the Flat Earth Society. Gun was proclaimed president and Content was elected treasurer of the international organization that was dedicated to the promotion of the obvious; the empirical truth that the earth was flat but not smooth. "No matter what, we got some wrinkles way out on the edges," the liberal elders allowed, "but this earth is flat right down to that heartless sea." The trickster priest was the only member who had traveled more than twenty miles from the center of town; ten more miles out and the earth might have been thrown into orbit on the prairie.

"Damn, the church is back," shouted Gun.

"Back where?" asked Content.

"Here, we got our priest back."

"My God, never thought this day would come, fifty-four years since the last priest, and our marriage, and the last big storm," she whispered and turned the lock on the back door. She had not locked the door since the time three men had escaped from the state prison.

Gun and Content tiptoed on the gravel road behind the priest, who carried a black portmanteau and a pennant case. White Lies and Pure Gumption, two mongrels from the baronage on the reservation, barked in the weeds near the outhouse behind the chapel. The mosquitoes were heinous at dusk.

"Father, welcome back," said Gun. "Wait, that door hasn't been opened since the last priest was here," he warned as the priest turned the wide brass key in the lock. "When we took over, we used the back door all these years."

Angels carved on the oak panels cocked their weathered eyes and braced the double doors. Gun butted the center, then the priest pressed his shoulder on a rimrose breast and the two men beamed, but the doors would not open. The mongrels pawed and barked. Content waved the men and mongrels aside.

She pushed one side and pulled the other; the double doors screeched open and separated the spider webs that had sealed the cracked panels.

The chapel smelled of stale cigar smoke. The rose windows at each end were clouded over with webs and dead insects. Several red broadsides, nailed to a huge black patriarchal cross, announced the annual celebrations of the International Flat Earth Society in Fortuna. "Come to North Dakota, the Best Corner on the Edge." The trickster healer cleaned the windows and polished the cross.

Double Father transformed the chapel with herbs and wildflowers, common birds, and miniature windmills that his sister had built for the occasion. The chapel was a wild haven: birds nested in the wooden nave; mongrels healed on the communion table; and three windmills whirred and burred over the verdant chancel. The steeple was painted in rainbow colors and the chapel was christened the Cathedral of the Flat Earth.

Pure Gumption, the shaman mongrel who glowed and healed with her paws and tongue, inspired the priest more than dead letter supplication and absolution. This mongrel, who was abandoned on the baronage and ran with White Lies, taught the trickster the animal art of healing with the paws.

That summer the lonesome and sick came over the prairie to be healed by the shaman mongrels and the crossblood priest. There were hundreds of families camped near the river and on the distant meadows. The trickster demonstrated how to scream into panic holes; at night the voices carried to the chapel and the bedrooms in the town. Content cursed the wanderers and closed the windows. "Sick people," she whispered to her husband, "sick and lonesome howlers like the rest of us in this dead town."

Double Father and the mongrels praised the lonesome on

the run and healed the sick in the chapel when the sun dropped over the edge of the earth. The natural time to heal was at dusk when the trees, birds, and animals spread their enormous shadows.

Pure Gumption glowed on the communion table; she laid her paws on the lonesome and licked the sick. On the other side of the chancel the priest liberated and healed the animals and birds that were penned inside the humans. White Lies moved down the narrow pews and pushed her wet nose under dresses, into moist groins. The elders scratched her head, and she smiled and licked their arthritic thighs; the touch of a mongrel lowered their blood pressure, which had been elevated by guilt and television evangelists.

One humid evening the low sun bowed through a rose window and severed the communion table. The birds twittered in the nave and swooped down on the mongrels; the air cavities in their bones were sensitive to the approach of a storm. Thunderclouds billowed in the distance and towed ominous shrouds over the prairie.

The wind roared, and the nave beams strained. Wild lightning sheared weeds on the meadow, and thunder boomed in the chapel. The priest herded the sick and lonesome to a dark storm shelter. There, the mongrels barked at the thunder demons, and the humans told stories until the storm had passed.

The Cathedral of the Flat Earth lost a few wooden staves from the steeple, and the outhouse was overturned, but there was no real harm. However, trees were down, and most houses in the town were ravaged by the storm. Windows were shattered, trailers were overturned, and the water tower listed to the east.

Gun and Content summoned members of the Flat Earth Society to witness the damage; the wind had moved their small house several inches on the foundation. The water and sewer pipes were twisted and exposed; there were minor leaks, but no breaks.

"Help me move it back on the foundation," shouted Gun. He shivered over the words, and his bleached cheeks trembled with fear. "Help me, do something."

"Bulldozers, we need some machines."

"No, house jacks might do it."

"We can push," said Double Father.

"You caused us enough trouble," he moaned. Gun glanced at the older members and nodded his head. "This is my house, not the chapel, so leave it to me."

"We never had a storm this bad before, not since the last priest was here," said the manager of a gasoline station. He turned his head and held one ear.

"Never, never this bad," shouted Content. She was perched on her elbows at the bathroom window. "Father, you and those wild mongrels brought us some real bad luck this time."

"You said it," chimed the others.

"First, those strangers come here for some cure, and now this storm," said Gun. "Father, you best stand aside now; this is a man's job."

"But this is the Flat Earth Society," pleaded the priest.

"Not anymore," said Gun.

"We just had a vote and changed the rules," said Content. Her voice vibrated on the plastic window screen and released rainwater from the squares.

Double Father was wounded by the sudden rescission of his membership in the Flat Earth Society. He moved back with the mongrels and listened to the men discuss the methods to restore the house. While the men measured the distance to the nearest stout tree, an anchor for a house jack, the priest touched the mongrels. His hands were warmed, his breath was heated, slow and determined.

Pure Gumption glowed in the wet weeds behind the house. White Lies bounced in circles and barked into shallow panic holes. The Flat Earth Society members shooed the mongrels and continued their measurements.

The crossblood healer placed his hands on the corner of the house, pressed his shoulder to the wet clapboard, and pushed with the power of an old tribal shaman. His hands glowed on the rough boards, and the house shuddered. Pure Gumption butted the back of his legs and pawed his heels. White Lies barked at the white light that surrounded the trickster and the corner of the house.

"What the hell is he doing?" asked Gun.

"He's pissing on the corner."

"No, he's possessed."

"What the hell is this? Call the state patrol!"

"My God!" screamed Content.

"Jesus Christ."

"Wait, wait," shouted Gun. "Listen to that, the house is moving, that crazy priest is moving our whole damned house back on the foundation!"

The windows trembled, the walls shivered, and the floor joists roared as the crossblood pushed the house back several inches on the foundation. Mosquitoes swarmed the silent men behind the house. Content locked the windows and doors; she tested the toilet and hid behind the blinds.

Later, the members of the Flat Earth Society gathered at the chapel to apologize to the priest. The double doors were locked, so the members entered at the back. The inside smelled of cigar smoke, as it had before the priest arrived. The birds and their nests in the nave were down. The plants had vanished, and the rose windows were clouded once again with spider webs. The black patriarchal cross folded a double shadow over the communion table. The trickster priest had tacked a hand-printed message on the cross; he invited the members to "heal the lost and lonesome, mend the houses last, and no priest will ever bother you again."

The Last Lecture

FATHER Mother Browne renounced the priesthood and returned to the baronage, where he became a public mourner and
a celebrant at funerals on the reservation; he was inspired by the
spontaneous paternosters and entreaties at tribal wakes, over the
panic holes and graves. The survivors besought the dead to remember a better past, humor over disease, mythic stories over
incurious studies, a woodland renaissance.

Father Mother mourned through the winter, and then on
the summer solstice he was moved in a dream to ordain a tavern
and sermon center. The Last Lecture was built on a watershed
below the scapehouse at the south end of the baronage. The urban crossbloods who had moved back to the reservation were
summoned to carve a stone precipice named the Edge of the
White Earth, behind the tavern. There, seven modern telephone
booths with double doors were mounted in a row; one opened
over the precipice. Those who subscribed to step over the edge
were allowed one last call before they dropped into their new
names and social identities.

"There ain't no such thing as a last lecture," said the postman, who was troubled over the increased mail service to the

baronage. "My wife says something like that. She says, 'These are my last words,' but she never means it."

"The last lecture, one at a time," said Father Mother.

"If you don't mind me saying so," said the postman as he cocked his hat, "you people are a strange lot with those booths, that scapehouse with the animals, and now this place."

"Shakespeare said that once."

"Did he now."

"In his last lecture," said Father Mother, "he listed one by one all the strange things he saw around him. Once he saw it and named it in a play, that was the end of it, nothing more to say."

"Well, he was onto something there, but he never delivered the mail to this place," said the postman. "If you start something else out here, make it the last letter."

The Last Lecture was a circular cedar structure with a bar and booths on one side, and a theater with tables and chairs on the other. Visitors were invited to present their sermons and last lectures on the theater stage. Crossblood educators, tribal radicals, writers, painters, a geneticist, a psychotaxidermist, and various pretenders to the tribal crown took the microphone that summer and told the bold truth; these lost and lonesome crossbloods practiced their new names, made one last telephone call to their past, and then dropped over the edge into a new wild world.

Marie Gee Hailme was dressed in paisley velvet and black lace when she raised the microphone to deliver her last lecture; her narrow mouth moved in a monotone. More than a hundred tribal people from communities on the reservation had crowded into the sermon center to hear the director of urban tribal education, the first to unburden her vanities that season; even the postman was at the bar that night. Marie Gee mumbled that the tribal values she had introduced in classrooms were amiss and biased.

"My skin is dark," she whispered, "you can see that much. But who, in their right mind, would trust the education of their children to mere pigmentation?" Marie Gee held the microphone too close to her mouth; her voice hissed in the circular tavern. "Who knows how to grow up like an Indian? Tell me that. And who knows how to teach values that are real Indian?

"I was orphaned and grew up in a church boarding school, so they trusted me, because of their guilt over my dark skin, and put me in charge of developing classroom materials about Indians," she said and lowered the microphone.

"I went all over the state lecturing about Indian values to help white teachers understand how Indian students think and why they drop out of school. But once, right in the middle of a lecture, an Indian student asked me, 'What kind of Indians are you talking about? There aren't no Indians like that out here on our reservation.' I realized right then that I was describing an invented tribe, my own tribe that acted out my hang-ups, which had nothing to do with being a person stuck in a public school.

"I was telling white teachers that Indians never look you in the eye and Indians never touch. Can you believe that I was teaching that as the basic values and behavior of Indians? Those weren't values; they were my hang-ups, and they had nothing to do with anybody else. My pigmentation and degrees made me an expert on Indians. Would you believe that my dissertation was on Indian values? My hang-ups became the values, and then I compared them to other cultures. White academics loved it, the whole thing made sense to teachers, but it had nothing to do with Indians, because the Indian students never understood what I was saying about the values imposed on them.

"So, I pulled back, turned around last month, and looked at myself and the other Indian teachers, at what we had been doing, and I discovered the obvious," she said in the same tone as she loosened her padded velvet coat. "We were all cross-bloods, some light and some dark, and married to whites, and most of us had never really lived in reservation communities. Yes, we suffered some in college, but not in the same way as the Indian kids we were trying to reach, the ones we were trying to keep in school when school was the real problem. But there we were, the first generation of Indian education experts, forcing our invented curriculum units, our idea of Indians, on the next generation, forcing Indian kids to accept our biased views.

"That curriculum crap we put together about Indians was just as boring and inaccurate as the white materials we were revising and replacing. We pretended to do this for Indian kids, in their interests, but were we really honest?"

"Never, no, never," a man shouted at the bar.

"I think not. We did it for the money and the power bestowed on us by liberal whites. We should have trashed the schools, not ourselves with the delusion that we were helping Indian students. We were helping ourselves and the schools hold on to their power over children, and all the while we pretended to teach Indian pride. Can you believe that?"

"Pride quit school with me," the man shouted.

"Compromise, the kind that leads to self-hatred, is what we were really teaching. I should have listened, the Indian kids knew better, but we used them to do good and get ahead.

"So, here I am, giving my last lecture, and tomorrow I'll walk over the Edge of the Earth with a new name and a bus ticket to a crowded place out by the ocean for a new start at my life," she said and tapped her finger on the microphone. "Thanks to

Father Mother, I'm through with my ideas about Indian values and education. Too much of that crap would kill an ordinary spirit."

Marie Gee saluted the crowd with the microphone; she bowed to the former priest, and then ordered a round of drinks for everyone in the Last Lecture. She was applauded and cheered at the bar; two stout men in a booth raised their straw hats in the seven directions and ordered seven more bottles of beer.

Coke de Fountain waited at the bar in silence; his massive shoulders shuddered when he listened to the educator end her career. He ordered a double gin and then entered his name on the roster as a last lecturer. The crowd roared with derision when his name was printed on the board above the noted author Homer Yellow Snow and several other last lecturers scheduled for that night.

De Fountain was an urban post-tribal radical and dealer in cocaine. His tribal career had unfolded in prison, where he studied tribal philosophies, and blossomed when he was paroled in braids and a bone choker. He bore a dark cultural frown, posed as a new colonial victim, and learned his racial diatribes in church basements. Radical and stoical postures were tied to federal programs. The race to represent the poor started with loose money and ran down to the end with loose power. When the dash was blocked, the radical restored his power over the poor with narcotics; he inspired his urban warriors with cocaine.

Father Mother waved his hands and called attention to the importance of last lectures. "Our next lecturer, the second in line, needs no introduction. You have heard his crossblood wrath in the cities, you have seen his wild face on television, and some have whispered his name in anger. Now, on our stage, the man who took the most and gave the least back, the mad deacon of the urban word warriors, has agreed to deliver his last lecture on the run."

Coke cleared his throat, a demonic rumble, and squeezed loud clicks from the microphone with the rings on his scarred fingers. The audience hissed and sneered and then waited in silence; bottles, mouths, and hands were cocked to listen.

"Wounded Knee was the beginning in our calendar, the first year of the new warriors," he roared as he pounded the microphone in his hand. "We went back and took that place, it was ours, the chapel and the graves. We earned it back, and we did it for the elders, so the elders could be proud again."

"Bullshit," a woman shouted from a booth.

"We always listen to our elders," Coke shouted back and waved one hand in a circle. "We did what the elders wanted us to do, we protected their sacred traditions."

"You did it for the money and the blondes," said an elder at the bar. He laughed at the radical and mocked his hand movements. "Money and women, that's why you went to Wounded Knee and that's what will put you back in prison, because you never did anything for anybody."

"Our young people are destroyed in racist schools," he roared, and he sputtered and moved closer, with the microphone pressed on his mouth like a rock singer. "Who are you to tell me anything? What have you ever done to save our children?"

"Wounded Knee we will remember," said the elder, "but you and your mouth, we want to forget. We want to forget what you have done to our memories."

"De Fountain, he's the one who saved our children with drugs and taught them how to hate," said a tribal woman at a table close to the stage. She turned and shouted to the others,

"This man never saved anyone, not even himself. He's evil, he hates himself, he's got no vision, he's a killer of our dreams."

"My conscience is clean. . . ."

"Your conscience is cocaine," the woman screamed.

"I came here to talk about racism and genocide. Genocide!" he barked into the microphone. "What have you ever done but sit on a bar stool and bring disgrace to our sacred mother earth?"

"Your mother earth is a blonde," the tribal woman said, and then she moved closer to the radical. "You use women and pretend to love mother earth, but you would rather have a blond woman than live on a reservation. You let a white foster family care for your children while you parade around and hate whites. Why don't you take care of your own kids before you worry so much about mother earth?" The woman stood below him in the aisle with her hands on her hips and chanted, "Woman hater, woman hater."

"I don't have to listen to this," he moaned and moved back from the tables, a man in retreat. His power had eroded, and now he was alone, cornered in his own lecture by those who had waited in silence on the reservation. "Wounded Knee told the world that we were proud people once again, and we did that for you. We saved our children from the disgrace of white racism."

"Wounded Knee saved you, no one but you and your pack of worthless downtown warriors," said the elder at the bar. "You can't even save your own red ass without a white lawyer, federal money, and now that damn microphone."

"Listen here," he bellowed and aimed the microphone at the old man. "I don't have to give my last lecture here, so pack up your backward ideas and forget it. Down your beer old man and forget it. You've got no pride, there's nothing left in you."

Coke de Fountain dropped the microphone on the floor, and

the sound rumbled in the tavern. "This is not my last lecture. Never, never," he told Father Mother. "Why should I give my last lecture to those tomahawks?" Coke threw the envelope with his new name at the crowd. He sneered over his shoulder on the way out, slammed the door, and hurried over to the confession booths at the scapehouse.

The Patronia Scapehouse was a haven for lonesome, wounded, and abused women in search of solace on the reservation. Near the entrance to the scapehouse, at the base of the crescent on the baronage, there were four booths where women listened to the wild confessions of men.

Homer Yellow Snow, the spurious post-tribal author, arrived in a brown limousine minutes behind the radical who withdrew his last lecture. The author told his chauffeur, a muscular blonde, to wait for him on the road below the telephone booths at the Edge of the White Earth.

"Father Mother?" asked Yellow Snow.

"Not me," said the elder at the bar. "He's over there at a table, the one in the white suit and black collar. Would you believe that man was a priest once?"

"Would you believe I was once an Indian?" he asked the elder and then ordered a bottle of white wine to celebrate his wild conversion.

"No, but who asked?"

"No one worth mentioning," the author allowed.

"Yellow Snow, you're here," said Father Mother. He rushed over to the author at the bar. "Please, join us at a table before you begin your lecture."

"Do you have the documents?"

"The whole bundle," responded Father Mother. "Change

of names, driver's license, credit cards, voter registration, the new you over the last past."

Patronia retains certain civil records, as several treaties provide, such as birth, death, marriage, and divorce. The Last Lecture expanded these common civil records to include surnames, licenses, legal residences, and other documents demanded by those who deliver their last lectures on the baronage.

Homer Yellow Snow demanded three new names, a recorded tribal death in an auto accident, a wake, and burial of his past on the reservation. These were provided at a much higher cost than the usual admissions to the new world beyond the Edge of the White Earth.

"So, what's your new name?" asked Marie Gee.

"Not a chance," the author said with a nervous smile. "No one but my chauffeur will ever connect my new names to the past."

"What a pity, we might have pretended," she sighed.

"That's the theme of my lecture."

"Did you prepare your last lecture?" asked Father Mother.

"Yes, but on the way over I read it to my chauffeur and changed my mind," said Yellow Snow. "This time my last lecture will be spontaneous, and the prepared speech will become my press release, along with the notice that I was killed tonight in a tragic automobile accident."

"Death kits for the authors," said Marie Gee.

"Pretend Indians," he whispered.

"The late Yellow Snow," announced Father Mother. "We are honored to have one of the best-known tribal authors here to deliver his last lecture."

"Ladies and gentlemen," said the author, with the microphone in both hands. He wore turquoise bracelets, a thick silver belt buckle, and a double beaded necklace. "You are about to hear the last, or rather the first, honest words of Homer Yellow Snow, author, historian, tribal philosopher, and last but not least, a perfect pretend Indian.

"Within the hour, my friends, I will be dead on a reservation road, and the Indian author you thought you knew will step over the edge and become a Greek, an Italian, perhaps a Turk, but no more will I be your Indian."

"Spare me the heartbreak," said a tribal man in a booth with two blondes. "You never were anything to me, white or whatever you pretended to be."

"Let the man talk," said Marie Gee.

"This last lecture actually began several years ago when a crossblood writer questioned my tribal identity. He challenged an autobiographical essay I had submitted for publication in an anthology," said the author in a sonorous voice. His words were practiced, measured tones on time. "You see, my tribal identities were pretentious, my blood recollections were artificial at best, and this crossblood writer detected how impossible were my autobiographical experiences. He told the editor of the book to either correct or drop my essay.

"He saw right through my invented tribal childhood, he detected flaws in my asserted poverty, in my avowed tribal identities, and he was secure enough in his own experiences to challenge me. I should thank him for driving me to this, my last lecture.

"That was the turning point, the beginning of my revisions, double revisions since then, preparations for my last lecture, and now over the edge with my new names. I have Father Mother, this extraordinary man, to thank for an opportunity to start a new life with a proper public confession.

"Save for one or two academic skeptics, I had the entire

white and tribal worlds believing in me as a writer and historian, and eating out of my hand as a philosopher, especially when I raised foundation support for films and tribal seminars," he said and then paused to consider the audience. The ticktock of the tavern clock measured the silence. Two men in a booth peeled the labels from several beer bottles and rolled the moist paper into wads.

"What other culture could be so easily duped?" asked Homer Yellow Snow. "Listen, all it took was a little dark skin, a descriptive name, turquoise and silver, and that was about it, my friends. With that much, anyone could become an Indian."

"Whites are the real victims," the elder shouted.

"What about the white people?" asked Yellow Snow.

"Dupe the whites," the elder answered from the end of the bar. "We duped the whites more than they duped us, we even duped them to think they were duping us."

"Really," mocked the author.

"You duped yourself to pretend you were like us," said a woman in a booth. "You're the white, you're the victim, and that's your problem, not ours. So who's the dupe?"

"So there, my tribal friends," he said with hesitation, "you have my story, the adventures of a pretend Indian who published his way to the top with turquoise and a tribal mask, and all of you needed me, white and tribal, to absolve your insecurities and to convince the world that you were more than a lost whisper in a museum, more than a stick figure on birchbark or a faded mark on buffalo hide."

"Yellow Snow, hit the edge," said a disabled man at the bar. He wobbled between the tables with bottles in both hands. "This here is a real skin on your trail, and we got a claim to piss on some of that phoney blood, mister white eyes."

"If you knew who you were, why did you find it so easy to

believe in me?" the author asked and then answered, "because
you too want to be white, and no matter what you say in public,
you trust whites more than you trust Indians, which is to say,
you trust pretend Indians more than real ones."

Father Mother handed Homer Yellow Snow his bundle of
new names and identities and an invoice for conversion services,
and escorted the author through the back door to the booths and
the precipice. Yellow Snow telephoned his chauffeur, removed
his turquoise, bone choker, beads, and stepped over the edge
into the new world with three new names.

The Last Lecture served thirteen tribal pretenders and several hundred crossbloods in the first few months the tavern was
opened. Father Mother provided new names and identities
through the baronage for a nominal fee. The cost was so low,
and the last lecture such a solace, that some crossbloods returned
several times to unburden their new identities for an even newer
name; the last lectures, for some, became an annual ritual. Some
crossbloods, however, belied their own last lectures, balked at
the booth and the edge, and returned to their past with dubious
resolve and courage.

Coke de Fountain turned his resistance to a new name into
a competitive business. The racial freebooter opened the Very
Last Plea, a fry bread parlor and tribal dessert house, where he
provided new descriptive names, cocaine, and membership in a
radical urban movement named the New Breed.

Father Mother introduced each last lecturer and listened to
their conversions; he endured the returns and repetitions, but
one night he interrupted a genetic acarid engineer and delivered
his own last lecture.

See See Arachnidan, a crossblood recluse who had moved
back to the reservation, revealed the parasitic testicle ticks that

she had bred to attack authoritarian personalities: police officers, court officials, some teachers, and federal agents. "One testick bite causes a rare disease. In an instant, men stutter like rich liberals on the Fourth of July. My testicks are aroused by certain male hormones in groin sweat," she said as the microphone died. She was told to sit down and be silent.

Father Mother stared at the audience for several minutes, and then he delivered his own last lecture. "Listen, I have listened long enough to last lectures of the lost and lonesome. Now it is my time to choose a new name and walk over the edge," he said and placed the microphone on a chair. The audience cheered when he removed his black collar, white coat, and trousers. He turned in circles and then walked backward in his shorts and white shoes out the back door of the tavern.

Father Mother was the last lecturer at the Last Lecture; he wrapped himself in a plain brown blanket, entered the telephone booth, and called his mother at the scapehouse. The former priest laughed in the booth and decided to become a woman with a new name in a new wild world.

Bad Breath

MILDRED FAIRCHILD was convinced that bad breath caused cancer and disorders of the heart. Surrounded by bad breath, she measured the seasons on a calendar of private theories and moved west to teach at the government school on the White Earth Reservation in Minnesota.

"Inhale the sunrise," she told her sisters. "Pure breath is the path to a clean mind and body." Mildred was buttoned too tight, but no one ever heard her rave in the dark. She inhaled the sunrise and hummed near water. Twice a week she trimmed her nails on the back porch; she was clean and worried about her appearance, but she never searched her smile in a mirror until she moved to the reservation.

Mildred was fifteen when her mother died, the sudden victim of bad breath. She hummed at the river. Later, over the grave, she promised to serve the survivors: her father, a miserable politician who practiced admiralty law with a morbid fear of the sea; twin sisters who turned to a secret language; and an elder brother who mourned for six months and then disappeared. Mildred cooked, washed, gardened, attended to her sisters, searched for her brother, and studied to be a teacher, in that order, from sunrise to the back porch at dusk. She was practiced, she was clean.

Three years later she smelled cancer on the breath of her chosen professor, the poet with psoriasis. Late that summer she bought a rail ticket west to the wilds of the reservation.

"Christians must not solicit praise for their simple missions," she told her father and sisters at the depot. "Hence my promise to serve tribal children, while a proper sacrifice, must be held a secret."

"Dred, come back when you must, no one will know where you were," one sister said in a loud voice. "We know how to keep secrets."

"Catholic priests are not to be trusted," warned her father in a cloud of cigar smoke. "You know how we feel about them."

"Father, no need for that now."

"Beware of the savages," he complained.

"Indians, father, not savages," said Mildred. She was eager for the train to depart. "Take care of your feet and remember not to eat too much salt pork."

"No Catholics."

"Yes, father."

"Dred, promise me," he insisted.

"Yes, father."

"No savages."

"No, father."

"Dred, you could still teach here at the country school," said her other sister as the train lurched backward and then forward a few feet on the platform. "Remember me, send us picture postcards with the wilderness."

"No Catholics, promise me that."

"Yes, father."

"Dred, do you hear me?"

"Yes, father."

Mildred waved and waved from the open window as the train started and stopped several times at the station. No one could turn back at the right moment; last waves were hesitant, repeated, gestures were lost to the lurch of the machine.

Back in the spring of 1886 there sure was plenty of good excitement out here when the Beaulieus published their first newspaper on the reservation. White Earth has never been the same. Theodore, he had a cousin with the same name, and August, they tried all kinds of things from selling sewing machines to newspapers. Sewing was not a serious problem, but the words, little words with white around them, attracted the evils of the government. The way the agents saw it, reservation Indians weren't supposed to know anything about words, so it was the crossbloods that caused all the trouble. Government agents could cheat the fullbloods with words but not the crossbloods, and who were these mongrels who started a newspaper without permission? Printed words attracted the broken crows, and not far behind them was the old Indian agent Tipi Milcho. His real name was T. J. Sheehan, but we called him Tipi for the shape of his head and Milcho, well, I'm not really sure where we got that name, but we know what it means. Someone evil, I think, someone who gave an Irish saint some trouble and a good name.

The Beaulieus called their paper *The Progress*, dedicated, they wrote, to a "higher civilization." Now, can you imagine that bit of idealism in the middle of a federal trust reservation with an Indian agent strutting around like some sort of colonial monarch? Well, the Beaulieus took after old Tipi with a vengeance. This was one headline on the front page: "Is it an Indian Bureau? About some of the freaks in the employ of the Indian Service whose actions are a disgrace to the nation and a curse to the cause of justice. Putrescent through the spoils system." You must understand that the Beaulieus weren't writing for us on the reservation; we knew that and more. They were throwing those words like "putrescent" around for God-fearing people back east, back where Tipi comes from, some say. Anyway, the agent choked on those words, so we knew what they meant.

Tipi Milcho was at the door, and he said those were fighting words. More than that, he put the newspaper out of business. He took the printing press in the name of the government, made a few drunks into deputies, and then he ordered the Beaulieus out of town, even before sundown. We sat on the porch of the Hindquarters Hotel and laughed at the deputies trying to move an old printing press. They gave up, ink on their hands and clothes, marked by the government forever.

Listen, if you knew the Beaulieus as well as we did at the Hindquarters Hotel that day, you would know that no one tells that family to leave the reservation, no one. Not even the government. They weren't mean or anything like that, but they were part of a big and important crossblood family, the first to settle on the reservation, and they were Roman Catholics.

Tipi arrived at high noon at the big white Beaulieu house near the Mission Pond with half a dozen deputies hanging behind in the trees. Dummy Funday and his cousin Birch were up front with the agent; they both wore giant silver stars on their vests, the kind we saw in cartoons. The stars didn't change them much though; they still stumbled and stammered, always wanting to be in charge of something or another. Birch was white, he married a reservation woman. They were both pretty good boys, but they sure do hate Catholics, especially halfbreed Catholics. Tipi put together a pack of Catholic-hating deputies to run the Beaulieus out, but not one of them, not even the agent, had the courage to in the end. They came up the dirt path and stood for a long time below the porch stairs. The longer they stood there, the more people gathered on the road waiting for the action. Roman Catholics were the real enemies but nothing happened.

Tipi had started up the stairs of the Beaulieu place when someone in the crowd yelled, "Hey, watch out for the fifth step." So he stopped and looked around. He did look stupid with his pointed head and his sixgun at his side, playing the western hero, but he was really the loser, not a twig of humor in his bones. "The board is loose." We all laughed. Tipi thought the whole thing was a joke, and we knew he would, so he threw both feet onto the fifth step and fell on his ass down the stairs. He caught a sliver on his right thumb, drew some blood. We laughed again because it was his shooting hand, and we called out to him, "Tipi, watch out, those Catholics learn how to fast draw at confession."

Colonel Clement Hudon dit Beaulieu, the elder of the crossblood families, was at the door to meet his agent. He was no stranger, but even so, Tipi yelled his orders out: "You Beaulieus leave this reservation by order of the United States and the Honorable Secretary of the Interior." The whole government behind him and he was still scared. His voice was strained like a lonesome mongrel at a picnic. We never did hear what Colonel Clement said back to him through the screen door, but we could imagine it was worth a good confession. The old man wore a black morning coat; sometimes visitors took him for the priest. He had a real quiet voice, he was educated, and so were his boys. They all went to private schools out east somewhere. He was in the fur trade for a time, before the reservation was created. That's when the governor of the state made him a Colonel, but soon the fur was gone and the Indians were removed. He and his boys did the best they could as educated crossbloods on the reservation. They went into business, what else? They started a newspaper. The old man still tells a good story, he even plays a good poker hand, and he has a way with bears and horses. Better than most, he drinks with the priests.

Tipi kicked his heels at the door, looked down and around to see who was watching. We were sitting on the porch of the hotel watching him, and he knew it, so once more he ordered the Beaulieus to leave. Birch said later that Colonel Clement invited him over to the church and that scared him more than a shotgun aimed at his head. That's just what the Beaulieus did; they went over to the church, and Father Corner, that weird old man with a hatchet face, held a special service. The next thing you know, there was a United States Senate Subcommittee hearing about corruption at White Earth.

Listen, that was a long time ago, back in the good old days when words still had some power, so much power that government agents tried to remove the printing press on the reservation, and people sat around and laughed over their best stories. We laughed over that newspaper story many an afternoon, sitting on the porch of the Hindquarters Hotel.

Father Corner talked about the devil, but he never mentioned the government. Colonel Clement went all the way to Washington and testified at a hearing about corruption and the agent. Tipi Milcho never came back to the reservation, once the word was out. No one was surprised because he never should of been here in the first place. Tipi never laughed; everything was too serious to him. He even reported the doctor for dancing in the hospital and said that all the jerking around would weaken the foundation of the building and civilization. Dancing, now there's a way to destroy government property. Tipi never came back from the hearing, and the Beaulieus went back to publishing their newspaper, maintaining, as they said, our "higher civ-

ilization" on the reservation. Like I said, Colonel Clement had a
way with bears, and horses, and priests.

Father Laurence watched the sun crawl over the mount
named for Saint Columban, and then he plunged his narrow
head deep into cool water and thumped his fingers on the rim
of the wooden rain barrel. There, in that manner each morning,
he balanced his otherwise uncertain spiritual worlds under
water. He confessed that the resound, like the distant thunder
in tribal creation stories, stopped sacramental time; he de-
scended into a pacific sea.

Sister James, a conservative throwback to the old school of
pure and simple sacrifices, complained to Father Corner, whose
flesh was corrupt enough to retain a thin beam of humor, that
Father Laurence was possessed, that he had been touched by
"halfbreed savages and evil jugglers." She reported that the
young priest, new to the reservation and on his first appointment, chanted on the mount at night to "clear his unsettled
mind," talked to insects, and inhaled rainwater from a barrel at
first light.

"Father Corner, the wicked ones like him too much. They
ask him several times a day, 'How was your plunge this morning, Father?' and he says back, 'Just fine, thank you for asking.'
And he even smokes bark with those pagans at the hotel." She
confessed to her superior and then she explained that she had
passed these rumors to others, and she even told unkind stories
about the new priest to the sisters at the mission school. Sister
James had enormous feet, long and narrow, so narrow that she
ordered her shoes from a custom cobbler who supplied circus
clowns. She looked down at her shoes in the confessional and
noticed a thin crack in the leather. She tapped her toes together.

"Sister, this is your confession, not his," said Father Corner.

He was harsh at confession. He pinched his eyes closed and pictured the young priest on the loose. "Please, please continue the stories." She never failed to please the old priest with her wild and paranoid imagination; his curiosity and absolution each week were implicit.

"Father Laurence calls me Big Jim."

"So what? You confessed that last week," said Father Corner.

"He ridicules me."

Father Laurence was not sure how to answer the letter from Mildred Fairchild. She explained her situation in this manner: "The Bureau of Indian Affairs has employed me to teach at the White Earth government school, but the main office has not been able to provide me with information about the children or the reservation." He wrote a note to the Sister James, "Big Jim, please answer."

"No," she wrote back. "You be the expert."

"Dear Sister James," he addressed a second note. "Please, would you kindly answer the attached letter from Mildred Fairchild."

"No," she answered a second time. "Must we point out that Miss Fairchild is a federal teacher and we are a mission school?"

"Thanks again, Big Jim."

"Praying mantis have four thin legs," Father Laurence told Little Baron, son of Dummy Funday, and his little friend with no name. The two had been lurking all week in the woods behind his small house near the mission school. The tribal boys sought the attention of the new priest as an excuse to avoid their classroom teachers in the government school. Now, during the summer, Little Baron and his friend waited to time the priest in the rain barrel. The gamblers in the village started a secret cash raffle on how long the priest could keep his head under water. Colonel Clement Beaulieu loaned the boys his gold watch, the best one on the reservation, to keep the average time for seven plunges in the barrel. The fifth plunge was short, but the first four ran between three and four minutes. Colonel Clement believed that the new priest possessed unusual spiritual energies, so he bought each third second between three and four minutes. Imar Funday and his son Dummy bought the other marks on the clock, but for different reasons. Imar, who hates Catholics, was convinced that beneath the black robe of the priest there beat the black heart of an evil shaman. Others in the village, with much less cash on hand to risk, measured what the priest could do as a mortal white man. "Not much," said a woodcutter. He lost.

"Now, watch the neck. See there, see how it moves over the shoulder," said the priest as he touched the green back with a twig. The boys leaned on their elbows, close to the earth, to hear the lecture. The priest turned his head with the mantis, his face was round and tender, a hint of green from the trees. A scar creased his right cheek at the same level as his mouth. When the priest was twelve he chased a fawn across a field and caught his cheek on a barbed wire fence. "Mantis eat insects, and sometimes the female eats the male for dinner. What do you make of that?"

"I like dogs better," said the little boy.

"How long can you hold your head under water?" asked Little Baron, a crossblood with pale green eyes. He leaped to his feet, excited, and waited for an answer. A gray mongrel barked.

"Why do you ask?"

"We saw you in the barrel," said the little boy.

"Never thought about the time."

"We got a watch," said Little Baron.

"Where did you get that?" asked the priest.

"Colonel Clement gave it to us."

"Really?"

"We didn't steal it, we didn't," pleaded Little Baron.

"Well, I suppose you better time me with it then," said the priest. He brushed his black hair behind his ears and leaned close to the water. The boys waved their arms to mark the time, and the priest plunged his head into the rain barrel. One, two, three, four. . . . One minute, thirty-eight seconds for the sixth plunge beneath the water.

"You did better the last time."

"Never thought about it until now."

"Can we time you tomorrow?"

"Don't tell me about it," said the priest, and then he plunged his head into the barrel once more. The water was cool, he could hear animals at a distance, and then he pictured the new teacher at the window of the train.

"No, we won't," said Little Baron.

"Dear Miss Fairchild," the priest thought to write with his head deep in the rain barrel. "Please forgive this tardy reply to your letter. . . . Where should we begin to introduce you to the unusual people of this reservation?"

At the beginning, but then where is the beginning of this tribal place? "In 1863 the Indian Office submitted a plan to unite the scattered tribes," he continued to write at his desk. Through three narrow windows he watched the poplar and the oak leaves shiver in the warm breeze on the mount at Saint Columban. "White Earth was established by treaty in 1867, and on June 14, 1868, the first Indians, most of them crossbloods, began to arrive at White Earth from Mille Lacs, Pillager. The Beaulieus and the Morrisons, two prominent fur trade families from the Old Crow Wing, were the first to be removed to the new reservation.

"White Earth was a beautiful forest then, quiet and clean beneath the tall red and white pines. It was a good place for the first settlers. The Indian knew himself better in those days than he does today, and he had the pride of being on his own good land, until the enactment of the Dawes Allotment Act of 1886, which led to the illusion of individual ownership of the land. The trees were cut to build cities, and a few men became wealthy and in their guilt built monuments in their names at a great distance from the stumps they left behind on the reservation. Now we measure who we are from what we have done to the Indians.

"White Earth village, which is where you will teach, was subdivided into small blocks and homesites. Some roads were paved, a water tower was erected, and there were even plans for a sewer system that was never completed, but things are much different now. . . .

"This, of course, does not tell you much about the people who live here today. Well, let me tell you two stories, which is the way most Indians explain their time to a visitor.

"The first is about two Indian boys—they could be in your class next year—who came by to see me this afternoon. Rather, they were lurking in the trees behind the house. God knows why, but they have taken an interest in one of my peculiar practices: in the morning I rinse my face outside in a rain barrel. The water is so soft. Well, the boys are up to something because they have been timing how long I keep my head under water. Little Baron, the crossblood grandson of the shaman Imar Funday, is quick and full of wit, and he reminds me of the tribal trickster we hear so much about here on the reservation. Naanabozho is his name, or her name, a sort of cultural hero who creates and contradicts classes, manners, and political authority. There are many tales of his growing and learning. His grandmother told him that when Indians first ate the meat of animals, who were then speaking the same language, the animals got together and decided to punish humans with diseases. The plants and trees, however, decided that the Indians had not been unkind to them so they agreed to offer humans the secrets of herbal medicines to cure diseases given to them by animals. A rational balance, but the trickster upsets the balance, if for no other reason than to keep people alert to their own survival and powers to heal. The crossbloods are the tricksters; they settle the new worlds in their own blood.

"The second story is about Saint Columban, a sacred place on the earth that I can see at this moment through the window. We call it the mount, a meadow near the pond, and it is marked by four poles that have been carved down to stubs in the past few years. Tribal people come from all over the state to touch the earth at Saint Columban and to cut sacred slivers from one of the posts. The slivers, and the earth there, some believe, will cure cancer.

"Saint Columban, and most of this reservation, is unlike any place I have ever known or dreamed about before. It is truly a sacred place on the earth; it is a place where some are touched by visions and where religions begin, and some end. White Earth, on the other hand, cannot be introduced. This place must be a collection of every changing trickster story, and the longer I am here, the more we seem to change each time a story is told.

"White Earth might be one of those transitional places on the earth where the past is never the same in the memories of the people who lived here. This reservation is a collection of crossblood stories."

Father Laurence imitated the water strider, he touched his

hands on the rainwater and moved on the surface. He could feel the tension there, but he was not small enough to walk across the rain in the barrel. He leaned over and rolled the reflection of his face from side to side with his hands and then he plunged his head up to his naked shoulders. He listened to the distance in the cool rainwater, his meditation at first light.

Little Baron, tucked behind a tree with the gold watch, timed the priest at three minutes, forty-two seconds. Imar Funday, his wicked grandfather, was the winner; but when others in the village learned that his grandson had been the official timekeeper, they withdrew their money from the raffle.

Colonel Clement Beaulieu paid the crossblood, made good on his bet as always, and then drove to meet the new schoolteacher. Perched high in the seat of his plain black motorcar, he confessed his basic needs to the priest.

"Basic needs?" asked Father Laurence.

"Education, women, priests, and red wine."

"No song?"

"I had no idea the new teacher could sing," he said and then burst into laughter. Colonel Clement looked around the fields; the slant of morning light raised the corn. He waited for the priest to ask the most obvious question.

"How many basic needs do you have?"

"Seventeen, at last count," he said.

"What might one or two be?" asked the priest.

"Not until you tell me how you can hold your breath for such a long time under water in that rain barrel," he said and leaned into a curve.

The broken road from White Earth curves near the Mission Pond, circles the mount, and then unfurls like a ribbon snake between the corn and alfalfa fields. Ogema is a white town on the border of the reservation; the nearest railroad depot, a place where the plains begin and alcohol is dispensed at a high price.

Mildred Fairchild stood beneath a pale blue parasol at the entrance to the Paradise Bank and Trust Company of Ogema. The church was hidden behind the public school, not obvious to a visitor. Mildred waited near the pillars of the bank, between her valise and a small trunk. She was tired, but she stood erect with her small feet close together on the broken concrete.

Her blond hair was bound in a loose bun low at the back of her neck. She watched the street, alert to the gestures of others. She did not know that there was more behind those mock pillars than a bank.

"Miss Fairchild, I presume," said Colonel Clement.

"Your name, sir?"

"Your chauffeur," he said and smiled.

"Your name, sir?"

"Colonel Clement Hudon dit Beaulieu, at your service."

"Do you live on the White Earth Reservation?" she asked and then folded her parasol. The blue cloth was faded and clean. She was nervous, insecure, and she avoided the priest.

"Indeed, since the night it was invented."

"What do you do there?"

"Twice retired," he said as he reached for the small trunk.

"Twice?"

"Fur trader once and farmer twice."

"My father is a lawyer," she said.

"So he is," said Colonel Clement as he walked to the car. "Perhaps you would not mind waiting here for a few minutes with Father Laurence while I conduct some business at the bank?"

"Not at all, Colonel." She settled in the middle of the back seat.

"Here is my response to your letter," said Father Laurence. He was standing outside the car and handed the unsealed envelope to her through the window in the back door.

"But I never wrote to you." Mildred hesitated and did not open the letter; she placed it beside her on the leather seat.

"Your letter was forwarded to me because the other teachers have left for the summer," he said through the window. She looked past him when he spoke. "Forgive me. . . ."

"For what?" she snapped.

"Forgive me for not writing to you sooner about what to expect here," he said in a slow and awkward speech. "When I finally took up my pen to answer, well, I noticed that you would be here before the letter could be delivered."

"Thank you."

"Did you notice the bank?"

"Well, of course."

"What I mean to say is, did you notice that the bank is more than meets the eye?" The priest rested his bare arm on the window. The black metal was hot in the sun.

"Not really." She turned toward the entrance to the bank. Her face came too close to his arm on the window, too close to the thin black hair that spread down to his fingers. She pinched her lips and moved back from the window.

"The bank is in the front, as you can see, but behind that is a liquor bar," he explained in a louder voice, "and behind the bar is a land trust company."

"My father would call that a western."

"Western, indeed," said the priest. He pushed his head through the open window. "They bank on one end, grab land, Indian land and valuable timber, on the other end, and then drink and celebrate in the middle."

"What would they think of me," she asked and leaned forward on the leather seat, "standing there at the door to the bar?"

"There stands the new schoolteacher," he said. "People seem to know just about everything around here; not much gained with a pose."

Katydids sounded in the trees. Mildred opened the back door and placed one foot on the runningboard. "Colonel Beaulieu, would he be a banker or a drinker?" she asked.

"Both, and he would agree."

"Father Laurence, would you show me the bank?"

"The bank?" He took her hand and watched her move from the car. He opened the door to the bank, stood behind her, and imagined that he saw her small bare feet move on the cool marble floor.

Mildred followed a path worn in the marble from the vestibule to the bright white entrance and to the bar in the back. Two men watched from behind brass enclosures at the side of the bank.

"Where is the bar?" she shouted.

"Through the back door." The priest pointed to a steel door that had been the entrance to the vault. The door handle, a wide copper wheel, had turned green. "Not a comfortable place for a woman."

"What could be so bad about a bar?" she said. Her shoes ticked on the marble, a determined measure. She never would have entered a bar at home, but this was a western, on the border of civilization, and she was moved to experience deceptions. She towed the green wheel and walked into the bar ahead of the priest.

The room was dark and smelled of mold and liquor, cigar smoke, and perspiration. Mildred pinched her nose at the masculine emanations, but it was the smell of bad breath that forced her against the wall. She gasped and retreated to the back seat of the car.

Father Laurence, meanwhile, heard his name mentioned when he entered the bar. He approached Colonel Clement, who stood at the end of the bar with several other men from town. The men talked about bankers and games, winners and lovers.

"Saint Laurence of the rain barrel," said one man.

"No saint could survive on this reservation."

"Much less around crossbloods," said another man.

"Laurence has been touched . . ." Colonel Clement stopped in the middle of his sentence. "Laurence, I would like you to meet some of my friends . . ." When the crossblood turned, the four men at the bar had disappeared. "Some people fear the best in a man."

"Mildred Fairchild. . . ."

"Father, forgive me, she was lost in the stories," he said and wrapped the opened bottle with several others in a small leather case. "She was under the stories."

"Colonel, would the game you mentioned to your friends at the bar be of interest to me?" The priest walked and talked to the bank entrance.

"Yes, it would indeed," said Colonel Clement. He covered his eyes from the bright light. "We bet on how long you could keep your head under water in that rain barrel."

"Little Baron borrowed your watch to time me then?"

"The average time for seven tries," he said and handed the leather case to the priest near the car. "Funday won, but the game died because the others would not trust the timer."

"But he is an honest boy."

"Fundays are honest to the seeds, but few trust them."

"People fear the dark," said Father Laurence.

"Miss Fairchild, forgive me, for we have sinned," said Colonel Clement. He started the engine, turned, smiled, and nodded toward the back seat.

"Priests and crossbloods are ritualists," he construed with a flourish. "We are the creatures folded in stories, better told, better remembered than morals and manners."

"Such ritual banking could be bad for your health," she said in a serious voice, but then she smiled and leaned back in the warm leather. She had removed her blue gloves.

"There you'll find a gentle argument," he said and started the engine. He slipped his hands into large gloves to handle the hot wooden wheel.

"Father Laurence?"

"Yes."

"Did you retrieve the letter you gave to me?"

"No, I thought you placed it on the seat."

"I am afraid the letter is missing," she said.

"Father, please see that her trunk is tied to the back." Colonel Clement turned and stopped the car. "Some people borrow too much in this town."

"Trunk is here," said the priest. He looked in the back seat, and under the seats. "Miss Fairchild, I am afraid that someone has borrowed your valise."

Colonel Clement reported the missing valise to the local constable and then, as best he could, assured the new teacher that the letter and her personal properties, nightdress and underwear, would soon be returned.

Mildred listened to the wind and smelled the hot timothy, corn, and meadow flowers. For a few minutes she was alone, for the first time in years, at peace in the back seat. Redwing blackbirds cracked the air on both sides of the narrow road back to the White Earth Reservation.

Mildred moved into a small private room attached to the back of the Hindquarters Hotel. The outside wall was stained, and the fleur-de-lis border paper had fallen near the corner. She pulled the lace curtains back and opened the windows on both sides; there was a trace of mold in the room.

She was tired; the breeze was warm and humid. She removed her shoes and stockings, loosened her dress, and leaned back on the misshaped bed. The linen was hard and clean, the pillow smelled fresh; she thought about her mother and burst into tears.

"Dred, come rest beside me now," her mother said in a dream. The linen was pure white and scented with clover. Mildred buried her head in the pillow and counted silhouettes until she was lost in sleep.

Mildred smelled bread fresh from the oven. She was home with her mother at last, but then she awakened; the linen was coarse, the wallpaper was stained and pared. She was alone on the reservation with savages late in the afternoon.

Two boys, one with cat-green eyes, stared at her from behind the window screen; one pressed his nose hard against the wire and crossed his fingers.

Mildred screamed; she pulled a blanket over her bodice, and then burst into tears a second time.

"There, there, nothing to fear now," said the hotel cook and baker who heard the screams. The stout brown woman lowered the blanket and soughed until the teacher turned a smile, however thin. "There, there, come with me now and we'll have some coffee and fresh bread."

"Thank you," Mildred said, and then she dressed. Her movements were slow, deliberate, she was ashamed to be alone and dependent on strangers, afraid that she would forget her name. She studied her face in the mirror, the irregular glass rolled her nose and cheeks flat. She tried to smile but each gesture brought silent tears. She had never come so close to her face in a mirror; she had avoided such vanities at home.

"There, there, nothing to worry about now. You'll be up in the new house with the other teacher in a week or so, as soon as she returns and they put in the water," she said with her hands on her wide hips.

"The room is fine really."

"There, there, never mind now," she said and held out her fat hand. "Mildred, is that what your mother called you at home?"

"Dred for short."

"Well, we'll just call you by your whole name," she said as they walked down the hall to the hotel kitchen. "My name is Gracie Bobolink, but my friends call me Greasie because I'm the head cook here."

"Greasie?"

"It's good to call me Greasie," she insisted with a wide smile. Two front teeth were broken. "Before that name they called me Beaucoup Bobolink."

"Bobolink?"

"Yes, my mother came down from Rat Portage with no name, and in those days government agents gave us bird names." Greasie chirruped.

"Greasie, I'm pleased to know you," said Mildred.

"See there, you feel better now."

"Yes. I was dreaming about my mother, she died eight years ago, and when I woke up I saw these two boys at the window. One of them had strange green eyes."

"That would be Little Baron, no trouble," said Greasie.

"Little Baron?"

"Nicknames, tumble names." She started to explain tumble names and then looked out the kitchen window. "Some people wear out their names and get new ones from time to time."

"Dred never wore out."

"Little Baron, come here, boy," Greasie called through the

window. When she moved, the flesh under her arms waved like a wattle. She held the back door open for the green-eyed boy. "What you got there?"

"Letter from Father Laurence."

"Well, who did he write to now?" asked Greasie.

"Letter for the teacher," he answered and handed over the unsealed envelope. He turned his head, looked to the corners of the room, hid his eyes.

"Look up now." Greasie held her hand under his chin. "Look up, let's see those bright green eyes." She pinched his cheeks, "Where's the smile in those eyes?"

"Where did you get this letter?" asked Mildred.

"My grandfather, he told me to bring it here."

"Who is your grandfather?"

"Imar Funday, he's a big shaman," answered Greasie.

"I came to the window with the letter." Little Baron raised his head and looked at the teacher in the same way he had watched her through the window screen earlier.

"Little Baron, will you be in my class at school?" Mildred leaned over a few inches, closer to his answer. He nodded that he would, his green eyes flashed around the kitchen like a mongrel. He stopped at the loaves of fresh bread and touched his fingers to his mouth.

Greasie gave him two thick slices of warm bread covered with lard and sugar, one in each hand. Little Baron nodded, and then he butted the door open with his head and ran out.

Mildred sat at the kitchen table and read the letter. She sipped coffee but stopped when several flies paraded on the rim of the cracked cup. She waved the flies from the table, from her hair, from the letter.

Greasie watched the white teacher read and wave; she swatted the flies around her with a folded newspaper. Mildred nodded her approval with each smack of the paper. When she finished the letter she smiled and counted seventeen dead flies on the bare table.

"Colonel Clement said someone would bring it back," Mildred told Greasie over supper. The valise was on the bed when she returned to her room that night.

"Funday returns things around here, whatever is lost or stolen," said Greasie with a mouthful of sweet peas. "He's the shaman and he knows where things get lost and what people think about, so watch what you think around him or he'll say your mind back."

"Shaman, is that a witch doctor?"

"You should ask the priest about that."

"My father told me to avoid Catholics." Mildred leaned on her elbows and waved her fork over the table, an unusual gesture. She heard an echo in her voice; she watched her gestures from the inside, the rituals from word to hand.

"The priests be good to me." Greasie made the sign of the cross and then she wiped her plate clean with a thick slice of white bread. Three fat black flies pursued her hand from plate to mouth and lost.

Thunderbirds overturned the prairie, and late in her dreams that night the bed trembled and the room blazed with lightning. Pillars of hail crossed the Mission Pond and hammered a barrel at the back of the hotel. The rain smelled of meadow flowers and twittered on the narrow wooden windowsills.

Lightning cracked at the tall white pine.

Thunder chattered at the panes.

Mildred lost her place in the world; the scenes beneath her hands burned. She told her mother to wait, whispered secret fears to her sisters, and then she called out her own name to be sure that she was there that night. Nothing returned; her voice was lost in the thunder.

The wild wind pulled at nests in the trees, turned signs around, tore shingles from the hotel. The ceiling in her room leaked over the bed and in three places near the windows. Drops of rain hit the brass headboard and splashed on her face, soft and cool.

Mildred imagined animals on the oil lanterns. There were bears at the windows, and an owl screamed from the bars at the end of her bed. A snake uncoiled and hissed from a corner near the ceiling. Her wet flesh tingled; thunder trembled in her pillow.

Mildred called out for Greasie, but her voice was lost. The room came alive and then died with the light; nothing could be darker. Images danced on her hands, on the walls, at the windowsills.

Shamans were at the windows.

Little Baron was a white cat in a flash of lightning, his green eyes blinked and splashed at the foot of her bed. She opened her mouth to scream but there was no sound.

Trees snapped on the hill behind the hotel.

Imar Funday appeared at the other window as a black bear with his front paws on the sill. Lightning flashed from his maw and sharp teeth, and his roar rattled the lanterns and shook the bed.

"There, there, never mind now. You are good," said Greasie. She touched the teacher's hot cheeks in the dark. "We get storms like this every few days in the late summer, thunderbirds from the mountains, the weather of the shamans."

"Greasie, they were here."

"Who was here?"

"Funday and Little Baron, at the windows."

"There, there. Funday is a shaman, he has the time of the night to go where he wants to. He was at my window once, he even moves in dreams," she said in a calm voice between the low rumbles of distant thunder. "Funday can scare the ears from a corn stalk, but he never hurt anybody. Sounds to me like he might have taken a liking to you."

"No, no, not me," pleaded Mildred.

"There, there, you'll just have to learn how to talk to a shaman at night and then you won't be scared." Greasie rubbed her hands together.

"How do you talk to a shaman?"

"The trick is not to see a shaman the way he comes out of the dark or in a dream," said Greasie. "Suppose he was at the window there, right now, I'll bet he would want us to see him as a bear?"

"Yes, he was a bear." Mildred seemed surprised.

"Well, there's one way to trick a shaman," she said as she leaned back to the foot of the bed. "Pretend that he's just a boy who showed his little brute at the dinner table, so you say to him, 'Funday, listen here, put that little thing away before the butcher cuts it up for sausage,' and that works because a shaman has sex on the brain, that's how he gets around in our dreams. So, if you cut his brute off, you cut the bear down to size."

"I've never thought like that before."

"You've never been on a reservation before either," said Greasie. The bed creaked when she laughed. "Try the brute removal sometime, you'll see for yourself."

"But there were other animals."

"What kind?"

"Crows, owls, cats, and a huge snake," she cried.

"There, there, you can talk to the priest tomorrow," said Greasie. She touched Mildred on the cheeks once more. Lightning flashed, but the storm had ended. "Crows, owls, and cats are the shaman, but you brought the snake with you on the train."

Mildred took a primrose to bed, and when the animals and birds appeared in her dreams later that night she touched them once on the head; the five petals transformed them into clean white moths. She inhaled the sunrise with the pure moths.

Funday appeared at the window once more, and when she touched him on the head he lost his black hair; he shivered at the window screen.

Little Baron waved into the room as a small bat, but he turned into a moth at the foot of the bed.

Father Laurence pressed his white hands, and then his cheek, to the small stained upper pane in the window. Mildred held the primrose high, she waited to touch the priest as she had the bear. Then, when the little priest danced through the window toward her bed, she swatted him several times on the shoulders with the primrose. The petals broke from the stem, and the more she swatted him the more he grew until she could see at her side the dark hair on his wrists and fingers.

"Miss Fairchild, are you all right?"

"Stay away," she screamed several times and beat the space around her bed with the wilted stem of the primrose. "Brute, brute, be gone."

"This is Father Laurence," he called. "The boys are gone."

"What boys?" Mildred was out of bed, behind the wardrobe near the door. She shivered, wrapped to her chin in a threadbare blanket. "Brutes at the windows, brutes on the bed."

"Little Baron and the others," the priest said in a gentle voice. He searched for the lantern in the dark. "Greasie Bobolink heard your screams and told me to look around outside. We wanted you to be comfortable, this, your first night on the reservation."

"Do you smell bad breath?"

"What breath?"

"Bad breath of death," she whispered.

"No," he said.

"Never mind now."

"Should I light the lantern?"

"No, don't do that," she said from behind the wardrobe. "Who was that at the windows, who was the bear out there?" Her voice was weak.

"Little Baron and his friends have a collection of animal masks," the priest said. "They stood in the windows with different masks."

"Bears and crows?"

"Yes, and other creatures."

"An owl?"

"Yes, owls, hawks, crows, the birds."

"Snakes?"

"That must be a new one."

"Who was the snake?"

"Miss Fairchild, there is no place you could be more secure than on this reservation," he lectured. "No one here will harm you. What has happened to you is what happens to all of us from time to time. We call it love burns from the tricksters."

"Funday, was he there at the window?"

"No, he never wears masks," the priest said. "He walks around in a blanket burnoose to hide the hideous scars from a burn on his cheek and neck."

"But he was there," she insisted.

"Miss Fairchild, would you like to walk with me around the village?"

He continued talking before she could answer. Her first answer would have been negative, but the more she listened the better she felt about his invitation. "This is the most beautiful time of the night. The thunderstorm has passed, silent lightning on the horizon, the air is clean and clear. The earth must have been like this at creation, at the first light."

"Thank you. . . ."

"The fresh air will do you good," he said before she could change her mind. "There is nothing to fear on the reservation, not even the shaman."

Greasie lived in a corner room on the second floor of the hotel. From there, she could see the government school, the mission, the pond below the meadow, the hospital, and the sacred mount in the distance. She could see them down on the road, the moon was bright, and later she heard their voices from the mount.

Mildred stopped beside the road and reached into her pocket. "Father Laurence, this is a silly thing, but I want you to see a picture of my father."

"I would be delighted." He turned the small photograph to the best light. She watched mosquitoes circle the moist clouds from his breath as he admired her father.

"My father hates Catholics," she said with her head down. "He warned me. Does that trouble you, that so many people hate you?" She looked at the picture of her father on the porch.

"Do you have an answer?"

"Where are we going?"

"There is a special place at the top of the hill," he said and pointed to the mount behind a stand of white pine trees. She turned to swat several mosquitoes on her neck and then on her ankles.

"Whose house is that?"

"Colonel Clement Beaulieu."

"The mosquitoes wait for my breath," she complained.

"There are no mosquitoes on the mount." He brushed his arms and neck. He heard animals in the distance. Lightning burned in the thunder clouds.

"One bit me on the forehead."

Father Laurence smiled and pointed to the mount. Mildred led the way on a narrow path through several bands of trees. First the birch and poplar and then the white pine. The grass was moist. She shivered under the pine closer to the mount; her sleeves were wetted, and her leather shoes were soaked. The wet cotton held to her breasts.

The mount, a natural meadow in the white pine, was covered with sweet clover. Mildred turned in circles, her arms extended, and the moon bounced over the branches. She twirled like a child until she lost her balance and tumbled on her side into the clover. She rolled over on her back.

"This is the mount." The priest was possessed on the mount.

"When I was a child my mother put clover in my pillow at night," she said and touched the moon in the white pine. "She told me that the blossoms would make my dreams sweeter. No bad breath in the clover."

"You could do that here."

"This is a beautiful place," she said and turned over onto her stomach, her chin in her hands. She had not noticed that the clover was warm, not wet, there was no rain on the mount.

"Naanabozho, the trickster, was the first to imagine this mount," he said and then sat down next to her in the clover. "The missionaries were the first to take the credit. They named the mount after Saint Columban."

"Never heard of either one," said Mildred.

"Neither had I until one night I came up here to watch a thunderstorm approach," said the priest. "The lightning and rain circled the mount, I could feel the moisture in the air, of course, but not the rain."

"How can that be?"

"Naanabozho, I was told, was transformed into four different animals and birds to protect his sick grandmother who was stranded on the mount during a thunderstorm. The trickster was a bear over there, a crow over on that side of the mount, and an otter and waxwing on the other sides. The four sides of the trickster stopped the rain one night, and the thunderbirds never forgot what happened."

"That's fantastic," she said.

"The missionaries believed otherwise," said the priest. "There are people who come up here to pick clover, find stones, or cut pieces of bark from the trees on the four sides of the mount. The stones and bark are spiritual medicine and heal."

"You wrote about that in your letter," she said. "Do you believe those stories about the trickster, the stones and the rest?"

"Life begins with imagination."

"How did you get that scar on your cheek?"

"I was a child when it happened," he said and rolled back in the clover next to her. "I was chasing a fawn, tripped and fell on a barbed wire fence, nothing more."

"You smile on one side."

Father Laurence imagined that he turned to the side and touched her cool moist shoulder, first with one finger and then with his whole hand. She moved closer and kissed the scar on his right cheek and then drew his head down on her low breasts. He listened to her heart beat and moved his hand across her warm stomach and down her thighs. She opened her legs to his hands. She touched his ear with her tongue and pulled the hair at the back of his neck, and then she squeezed the muscles down his back. She tore the cotton from her breasts and he sucked on her nipples.

He imagined how she moaned, writhed in the clover, and forced his hand down on her crotch. He reached lower and pushed two fingers into her wet vagina with a sudden movement. She rolled from side to side on his hand. Then she opened his black trousers and touched his penis. He shot in the clover.

Mildred imagined that the priest whispered his secrets to her on the mount. His breath was clean and sweet, and she could feel his smile in her loins. She wore no underwear; her nipples were hard. He touched her ears with his tongue, loosened her hair, and then he rose above her in the light of the moon and made love with her until the doves whistled at dawn. She carried clover blossoms home to her father.

Greasie listened to the voices of the priest and teacher late at the mount and remembered the time when she was seventeen, when Imar Funday caught her on the road one dark night and lured her to the mount, where he practiced what he called "animal love with a shaman." She removed her pink bloomers and roamed over the clover on her hands and knees while he circled the mount and leaped from behind trees and mounted her as an animal might. She remembered best the bear. She conceived a child that night with the bear, and from the night with the otter too, but she never forgot the wild mountain goat. Remember the beaver with his sharp teeth at the back of her neck . . .

She would be a bear and roam at night on the mount, under the whole moon. She would flash her silver maw and hold the priest in the clover until first light.

Landfill Meditation

CLEMENT BEAULIEU conducts seminars on Native American Indian philosophies, pantribal landfill meditation, environmental fantasies, wild animal languages, transcendental sounds, and talking and walking backward, one night each week at Shaman High University in Orinda, California.

The teaching trickster was late last week, and when he entered the classroom, conversations stopped in the middle of sentences. He removed his leather coat with unusual caution, walked backward moving his head from side to side like an animal at the shoreline, smiled, turned out the overhead fluorescent lights, and then waited near the open window in silence. There, in his visions, he followed the water moons backward over the mountains on familiar tribal faces. Traffic over the Golden Gate Bridge roared down the word maps and sacred place names in the distance.

Beaulieu told stories backward about the four directions and the four tribal characters who traveled with him that night from the window: Martin Bear Charme, the outward meditator; Happie Comes Last, the demure backbiter; Oh Shinnah Fast Wolf, the metatribal moralist; and Belladonna Winter Catcher, the roadwoman of terminal creeds, the daughter of a shaman and a public health nurse. This is an interpretive translation from the *drawkcab* or backward patois, in which these stories were first told and recorded.

"Martin Bear Charme owns a reservation," the teaching trickster told backward in the darkness, "teaches a seminar on refuse meditation, and circumscribes his unusual images and wise transformations in the material world on a refuse mount."

Charme is motion, he has no pose; he commands the old world to understand that imagination and meditation are real in our own trash. He walks backward through the refuse and tells visual stories to writers who never take notes; he wanders to be considered, but never speaks to be recorded or smiles to be photographed.

"Words are rituals in the oral tradition, from the sound of creation, the wisps of visions on the wind," said the old tribal scavenger to his students in the refuse, "not cold pages or electronic beats that separate the tellers from the listeners." Landfill meditation restores the tribal connections between refuse and the refusers.

Charme, the crossblood master meditator who told that he wandered backward down from the Turtle Mountain Reservation in North Dakota, is much more vain than astute about his photogenic face and emulsion visage. He has an enormous nose, and his stare is blurred with motion, the power of the bear.

Last month at the Unitarian Church in Berkeley, Oh Shinnah Fast Wolf, autonomous mistress of metatribal ceremonies, sighed onstage, under the sounds of automobile traffic, about the guardians at the heart of mother earth, while a disciple, bearing a pacific smile, held open the double doors for one more cash contribution to balance the earth.

Happie Comes Last, reservation born nurse, public health

graduate student, and columnist for the *Mountain Meditator*, a critical tabloid on meditation and holistic healing, would have been the last cash donor, but there at the double doors, sorting through the cards and letters in her leather pouch like a marsupial, she found a free press ticket and a caricature of the refuse meditation leader. Flashing the ticket and caricature, she asked the disciple, as she moved beneath his outstretched arms, "Where is that refuse meditator parked?"

"Charme sits over there," the disciple said as he pointed with his blond head. "He would be in the white pants, the one with the shine on his nose, in the back near the window."

Comes Last leaned back to backbite with the disciple, asking, "Did you know that he walks and talks backward and he never answers interviewers but in public places like this?"

"No, never heard about that before," he whispered over his shoulder. "Where are his private places?"

Martin Bear Charme, founder of the Landfill Meditation Reservation and the seminar with the same name, scooped the oil from his outsize nose with his dark middle finger, his habit once or twice an hour, and spread the viscid mounds over his cuticles. Sitting near the window, one would never know, watching his smooth hands in backward speech, that the refuse meditator was reservation born, once poor and undereducated for urban survival.

Nose Charmer, his tribal nickname on the reservation, hitchhiked to San Francisco when he was sixteen, settled in a waterfront hotel, and studied welding. But scrap connections bored him, so he turned his attention to scavenging and made his fortune hauling trash and filling wetlands with urban swill and solid waste. His meditation reservation was once a worthless mud flat that he bought with a federal loan and covered with waste. Now his lush refuse reservation on South San Francisco

Bay near Mountain View is worth millions. Charme has petitioned the federal government for recognition as a sovereign
meditation nation.

"There was never refuse like this on reservations," he told
his seminar, because, he said, walking backward to the window,
"on the old reservations the tribes were the refuse. We were the
waste, solid and swill on the run, telling stories from a discarded
culture to amuse the colonial refusers. Over here now, on the
other end of the wasted world, we meditate in peace on this landfill reservation."

The blond disciple dropped his arms, and his smile and the
double doors wagged closed on the traffic sounds. Oh Shinnah,
her hair bound back in tight braids, cut countershapes around
her head in abstruse hand rituals and then snapped two match
heads together four times, igniting a small cedar bundle in front
of her on the floor.

Comes Last, smiling and nodding with embarrassment,
broke through the silent aisles while the little chapel filled with
thick, sweet smoke. Down the back row she cleared her throat
twice and then perched on a backless chair at the end of the aisle;
there, in the shadows, the old scavenger commanded the last
place near the window.

Charme scooped his nose oil once more while Oh Shinnah
focused on the visions in her crystal ball, and then, in perfect
tribal trickster time, he rolled with his chair past Comes Last in
magical flight toward the window, a movement she later described in her column as "soaring backward on a shaman chair."

Comes Last, startled by his soaring, dropped her pouch and
properties. Bending over to retrieve her press ticket and the caricature of the meditator, she snorted with shame and snapped
at him from the wooden floor, "Who the hell is this wanaki wanaki?" She remembered the first time she called on the refuse

meditator at his urban reservation. When she asked him about his education and his theories on meditation, he roamed in a room filled with trash. He said nothing more than "Wanaki nin wanaki." The cedar silence was broken by her loud and nervous voice.

Martin Bear Charme smiled, nodded four times backward, and then laughed, throwing his nose back like a bear at the tree line, ha ha ha haaaa.

Looking up from her crystal and turtle fetish, Oh Shinnah stopped her invocation on mother earth between the words "intuitive" and "compassion" to explain that she had serious business on her mind and in her heart, to which the blond disciple nodded his head in agreement, business about mineral companies and progressive reservation governments. And she said, "We will compete with children for attention during these ceremonies, but we will not compete with adults and animals. Send the animals out now, this is not a pound."

"Wanaki nin wanaki ha ha ha haaaa," Charme chanted, throwing his voice backward from his escape distance near the window. His voice seemed to come from the window.

"Who would believe you were a meditator?" Comes Last whispered out of the side of her mouth. She shifted from side to side on her chair. She was a bird who appeared perched wherever and on whatever she sat.

"What does it mean?" asked Comes Last.

"What does what mean?"

"Wanaki nin wanaki over and over."

"Thank god we are pagans ha ha ha haaaa," said Charme.

"Not pagan," she said, and her mouth tightened. "Not pagan. Tell the truth now, what does it mean, the ha ha ha haaaa?"

"Wanaki, a place of peace, nin wanaki, in me there is a place of peace, peace in our refuse on the wild mount, ha ha ha haaaa."

"Where?"

"Landfill and summer swill."

"Talk sense," she demanded, opening her notebook bound in leather and decorated with beads. "How are those words spelled?" she asked.

"DRAWKCABNAMAHS," spelled Charme.

"Mister Charme," she said, shifting her head to the side to see his nose, "what does it mean, landfill meditation?" She waited and then said, "Please, in a phrase or two, speak slow now."

"Unstable," said Charme.

"Unstable what?"

"Unstable in an earthquake."

"Be serious, please," said Comes Last.

"Stable."

"Stable what?"

"Stable in a mind swell," said Charme.

"Never mind," she said, closing her leather notebook. "Damn fool, what do you know about meditation?" she asked and then answered, "Nothing!"

"Refuse meditation cures cancer with dreams and visions, and some people clean their kitchens much better than others, too," said the solid waste magnate.

"Mister Charme, please, you are speaking to a registered nurse," she said and brushed lumps of leather from her black dress, "not one of your trash meditation victims."

Charme scooped the oil from his nose and continued. "Clean minds and clean kitchens are delusions, but when our visions are clean we seem to feel much better, but no less secure."

Comes Last turned her head to avoid the stare of the old meditator; she pretended not to be interested. "Stop talking at me," she said.

"Refuse to listen and you hear much better ha ha ha haaaa."

"Damn fool."

"Once upon a time taking out the garbage was an event in our lives, a state of being connected to action. We were part of the rituals connecting us to the earth, from the places food grew, through the house and our bodies, and then back to the earth. Garbage was real, part of creation, not an objective invasion of cans and cartons.

"Refuse meditation turns the mind back to the earth through the visions of real waste," the trash meditator continued. His voice distracted the celebrants sitting in the back rows. Heads turned, fingers were raised, and faces scowled. The old scavenger smiled back and resumed his stories.

"We are the garbage, the waste, we make it and dump it, to be separated from it is a cancer causing delusion," he said, but with some doubt in the tone of his voice. "We cannot separate ourselves, clean and perfect, from the trash we dump out back in the can. Clean is a vision of internal trash, not a mere separation."

"Stop this now," insisted Comes Last. "You made your fortune on trash and now you are making me sick with it. Leave me sit here now and not listen to you."

"Sickness is one of the best meditation experiences. Think about being sick, focus on your stuffed nose, make your mind an unclean kitchen," said the old scavenger. "Now, rather than hating to clean up the kitchen, making it smell different, get right down there with the odors. Focus on the stench in the corners, take the odors in, you know, the same way we smell our underarms, because we are the bad smells we smell, separated from our own real kitchens in the mind."

"What was that?"

"Never mind, the clean words that part us from the real smells leave us defensive victims of fetid swill and cancer. Ha ha ha haaaa, did you understand that part?"

"You are sick. What you need are some clean words in your head," said Comes Last. She moved two chairs down the back row out of his bad breath.

"Cancer is first a word, a separation without vision," he said and followed her down the row. "We are culture bound to be clean, but being clean is a delusion, a separation from our trash and the visual energies of the earth. Holistic health is a harmonious vision, not an aromatic word prison.

"Listen, we are the dreamers for the earth," he said in a deep voice. "Turning down the dreams with clean words, defensive terminal creeds, earth separations, denies odors and causes cancer."

The celebrants turned toward the old scavenger in the back row and told him to be silent. One woman wagged her hand at him, warning him not to speak about diseases during sacred ceremonies.

"We are death," said the refuse meditator to the woman in the next row. Unabashed, he stood and spoke in a loud voice to all the celebrants in the chapel. "We are rituals, not perfect words, we are the ceremonies, not the witnesses that connect us to the earth. We are the earth dreamers, the holistic waste, not the detached nose pinchers between the refuse and the refusers.

"Go to a place in the waste to meditate," chanted the refuse meditator. "Come to our reservation on the landfill to focus on waste and transcend the ideal worlds, clean talk and terminal creeds, and the disunion between the mind and the earth. Come meditate on trash and swill odors and become the waste that connects us with the earth."

"Pipe down in the back," said the blond disciple.

"Celebrate mother earth," said Oh Shinnah. She raised an eagle feather and told the mother earth celebrants that "the feather makes me tell the truth. Should I not speak straight, the feather will tremble. Now, listen, we live in a retarded country;

we vote for a peanut picker looking for a way to freedom, and look where we have come. People are tearing up our land without examining it.

"Hang with mother earth," she said and raised her fist. "If the four corners tribal land is destroyed, then purification comes with a closed fist. If the electromagnetic pole at the four corners is upset, the earth will slip in space, causing the death of two-thirds of the population, no matter where you go to hide."

"Oh Shinnah makes more sense with cedar smoke and fetishes than you do with all that double backtalk about meditation," declared Comes Last. She raised her chin and waited for the meditator to respond.

Silence.

The lights wavered overhead, flickered several times, and then went out. The celebrants whispered in the darkness until the smell of cedar smoke in the chapel turned to the odor of landfill swill, or what Comes Last described in her column as a "mixture of human excrement and dead animals." At first whiff the celebrants took cover in clean words, thinking the person next in row had passed bad air. But later, when the chapel filled with the scent of wildflowers, one celebrant allowed how terrible had been the smell. While the others praised the passing of the bad odors, Comes Last, whose nose had not separated from the world of animals, smelled a bear in the darkness.

Listen ha ha ha haaaa.

Martin Bear Charme moved around the chapel in the darkness, from row to row and chair to chair; he told stories about terminal creeds. His voice seemed to rise and waver from the four directions. Words dropped from the beams, sounds came from under the chairs, and several celebrants were certain that the stories he told that night were told inside their own heads.

Listen ha ha ha haaaa.

"Orion was framed in a great wall of red earthen bricks," said the refuse meditator. "Within the red walls lived several families who were descendants of famous hunters and western bucking horse breeders. The sign outside the walls said, 'proud people keep to themselves and their own breed, but from time to time we invite others to share food and conversation.'"

Belladonna Winter Catcher, who was conceived and born at the new tribal Wounded Knee, her traveling companion, Catholic Bishop Omax Parasimo, and several other tribal pilgrims knocked at the gate. "We are tribal crossbloods with good stories and memories from thousands of good listeners," said the tribal pilgrims. "Open the gate and let us in or we will blow your house down."

"Listen to this," said Belladonna. She read out loud the sign on the red wall: Terminal Creeds are Terminal Diseases. The Mind is the Perfect Hunter, and Narcissism is a Form of Isolation.

The metal portcullis opened, and several guards dressed in uniforms escorted the pilgrims through the red wall. The pilgrims were examined. Birthplaces and information about education, experiences, travels, and diseases, attitudes on women and politics, were recorded. The hunters and breeders welcomed the visitors to tell stories about what was happening in the world outside the walls.

The pilgrims followed the hunters and breeders through the small town to one of the large houses where dozens of people were waiting on the front steps. Introductions and questions about political views were repeated again and again.

Thousands of questions were asked before dinner was served in the church dining room. Bishop Parasimo was the first to shift the flow of conversations. He asked the hunters and breeders sitting at his table to discuss the meaning of the messages on the outside walls. What does it mean, "narcissism is a form of isolation? Please explain how the mind is the perfect hunter."

"Narcissism rules the possessor," said a breeder with a deep scar on the side of his forehead. "Narcissism is the fine art that turns the dreamer into paste and ashes."

"The perfect hunter leaves himself and becomes the animal or bird he is hunting," said a hunter on the other side of the table. He touched his ear with his curled trigger finger as he spoke. "The perfect hunter turns on himself, hunts himself in his mind. He lives on the edge of his own meaning, the edge of his own humor. He is the hunter and the hunted at the same time and place."

The breeders and hunters at the table smiled and nodded and then turned toward the head table where the bald banker and breeder was tapping his water glass. Belladonna was sitting next to the banker. Her nervous fingers fumbled with the two beaded necklaces around her neck.

The families applauded when the banker spoke of their mission against terminal creeds. "Depersonalize the work in the world of terminal believers, and we can all share the good side of humor," said the banker. "The terminal believers must be changed or driven from our dreams."

Belladonna could feel the moisture from his hot hand resting on her shoulder. He referred to her as "the good-spirited speaker who has traveled through the world of savage lust on the interstates, this serious tribal woman, our speaker from the outside world, who once carried with her a tame white bird."

Belladonna leaned back in her chair. Her thighs twitched from his words about the tame white bird. The banker did not explain how he knew that she once lived with a dove. The medicine man told her it was an evil white witch, so she turned the dove loose in the woods, but the bird returned. She cursed the bird and locked it out of her house, but the white dove soared in crude domestic circles and hit the windows. The dove would not leave. One night, when she was alone, she squeezed the bird in both hands; the dove was content in her hands. She shook the dove. Behind the house, against a red pine tree, she severed the head of the white dove with an ax. Blood spurted in her face. The headless dove flopped backward into the dark woods.

"We are waiting," said the banker.

"Silence is my best start." Belladonna shivered near her chair and chased the dove from her memories. She fumbled with the beads around her neck. "Tribal values and dreams is what I will talk about."

"Speak up, speak up!"

"Tribal values is the subject of my talk," she said in a louder voice. She dropped her hands from the beads. "We are raised with values that shape our world in a different light because we are tribal, and that means that we are children of dreams and visions. Our bodies are connected to mother earth, and our minds are the clouds, and our voices are the living breath of the wilderness."

"My grandfathers were hunters," said the hunter with the trigger finger at his ear. "They said the same thing about the hunt that you said is tribal, so what does tribal mean?"

"I am different than a white man because of my values," she said. "I would not be white; I would never want to be white, not even part white."

"Do tell me," said an old woman breeder in the back of the room. "We can see that you are different from a man, but tell us how you are so different from white people, from the rest of us here?"

"We are different because we are raised with different values," said Belladonna. She fumbled with her beads once more.

"Our parents treat us different as children. We are not punished, and we live in larger families and never send our old people to homes to be alone. These are some things that make us different."

"More, more," the banker and breeders shouted.

"Tribal people seldom touch each other," said Belladonna. She folded her hands over her breasts. "We do not invade the personal bodies of others, and we do not stare at people when we are talking," she said with more confidence. "Indians have more magic in their lives."

"Wait a minute, hold on there," said a hunter with an orange beard. "Let me find something out here before you make me so different from the rest of the world. Tell me about this word 'Indian' you use. Tell me which Indians are you talking about, or for, or are you talking for all Indians?"

"And if you are speaking for all Indians, then how can there be truth in what you say?" shouted the woman breeder in the back of the room.

"Indians have their religion in common," said Belladonna.

"What does 'Indian' mean?"

"Are you so stupid that you cannot figure out what and who Indians are?" snapped Belladonna. "An Indian is a member of a tribe and a person who has Indian blood."

"But what is Indian blood?"

"Indian blood is not white blood," she shouted.

"Indians are an invention," said the hunter with the beard. "You tell me that the invention is different than the rest of the world when it was the rest of the world that invented the Indian," he said. "An Indian is an Indian because he speaks and thinks and believes he is an Indian. The invention must not be too bad because the tribes have taken it up for keeps."

"Mister, does it make much difference what the word 'Indian' means when I tell you that I have always been proud that I am an Indian?" asked Belladonna. "I am proud to speak the voice of mother earth."

"Please continue," said a breeder.

"Well, as I was explaining, tribal people are closer to the earth, to the meaning and energies of the woodlands and mountains and plains, and we are not a competitive people like the whites who competed this nation into corruption and failure," said Belladonna.

"When you use the collective pronoun, does that mean that you are talking for all tribal people?" asked a woman hunter with short silver hair.

"Most of them."

"How about the western fishing tribes, the old tribes, the tribes that burned down their own houses in potlatch ceremonies?" asked the hunter.

"Exceptions are not the rule," said Belladonna.

"Fools never make rules," said the woman with silver hair. "You speak from terminal creeds, not as a person of real experience or critical substance."

"Thank you for the meal," said Belladonna. She smirked and turned in disgust from the hunters and breeders. The banker placed his moist hand on her shoulder once more. "Now, now, she will speak in good faith," said the banker, "if you will listen with less critical ears."

"Does she want a debate?"

"Give her another good hand," said the banker with the moist hands. The hunters and breeders applauded his gesture. Belladonna smiled and accepted what she thought were apologies; she inhaled and started over.

"The tribal past, our religion and dreams and the concept of mother earth, is precious to me, because living is not important if it is turned into competition and material gain," she said. "Living is hearing the tribal wind and speaking the languages of animals, and soaring with eagles in magical flight.

"When I speak about these experiences it makes me feel powerful, the power of tribal religion and spiritual beliefs gives me protection, because my tribal blood is like the great red wall you have around you. My blood moves in the circles of mother earth and through dreams without time, and my tribal blood is timeless, it gives me strength to live and deal with evil in the world," said Belladonna.

"Right on, sister, right on," said the hunter with the trigger finger on his ear. He leaped to his feet and cheered for her views. She should not have been so pleased with the applause of the hunters, bankers and breeders.

"Powerful speech," said a breeder.

"She deserves our best dessert," said a hunter in a deep voice. The hunters and breeders do not trust those narcissistic persons who accept personal praise.

"Should we offer our special dessert to this innocent child?" asked the breeder banker. "Let me hear it now, those who think she deserves her dessert, and those who think she does not deserve her dessert for her excellent speech."

"Please, no dessert," said Belladonna.

"Now, now, how could you turn down the enthusiasm of the hunters and breeders who listened to your thoughts here?" asked the breeder. "How could you turn down their vote for your dessert?"

The hunters and breeders cheered and whistled when the cookies were served. The circus pilgrims were not comfortable with the shift in moods, the excessive enthusiasm.

"The energies have turned evil here," said Bishop Parasimo up his sleeve. "What does all this cheering mean over mere cookies?"

"Quite simple," said the breeder with the scar. "You see, when questions are unanswered and there is no humor, the messages become terminal creeds, and the good hunters and breeders here seek nothing that is terminal, because terminal creeds are terminal diseases, and we celebrate the obvious when death is inevitable."

The families smiled when she stood to tell them how much she loved their enthusiasm. "In your smiling faces I can see myself," said Belladonna. "This is a good place to be. You care for the living." With that the hunters and breeders cheered once more.

"But you applaud her narcissism," said the bishop to the breeder with a scar. His hands were clean and folded in a neat pile on the table.

"She has demanded that we see her narcissism," said the breeder. "You heard her tell us that she did not like questions, different views. She is her own victim, a terminal believer."

"But we are all victims of our own words."

"The histories of tribal cultures have become terminal creeds and narcissistic revisionism," said the breeder. "The tribes were perfect victims, and if they had more humor and less false pride, then they would not have collapsed under so little pressure from the white man. Show me a solid culture that disintegrates under the plow and the saw."

"Your views are terminal," said Bishop Parasimo.

"Who is serious about the perfections of the past, and who gathers around them the frail hopes and febrile dreams and tarnished mother earth words?" asked the hunter with the scar. "Surviving in the present means giving up on the burdens of the past and the cultures of tribal narcissism."

Belladonna nibbled at her sugar cookie like a proud rodent. Her cheeks were filled and flushed. Her tongue tingled from the tartness of the cookie. In the kitchen the cooks had covered her

cookie with a granulated alkaloid poison that would soon dissolve. The poison cookie was the special dessert for narcissists
and believers in terminal creeds. She was her own perfect victim.
The hunters and breeders have poisoned dozens of terminal believers in the past few months. Most of them were tribal people.

Belladonna nibbled at the poison dessert cookie, her polite
response to the enthusiasm of the people who lived behind the
wall. She smiled and nodded to the hunters and breeders who
all watched her eat the last crumb.

The sun had dropped beneath the great red earthen wall
when the pilgrims passed through the gate. Belladonna and the
pilgrims were silent; they walked through the shadows. Seven
crows circled them on the road until it was dark.

"My father took me into the sacred hills," chanted Belladonna. "We started when the sun was setting because Old Winter Catcher had to know what the setting sun looked like before
he climbed into the hills for the night. The sun was beautiful, it
spread great beams of orange and rose colors across the heavens.
My father said it was a good sunset. No haze to hide the stars.
He said it was good, and we climbed into the hills. I can feel that
time now, I feel like we are climbing into the hills for the visions
of the morning."

"Backward?" asked Bishop Parasimo.

"We walked up part of the hill backward," said Belladonna.
She turned her head backward. "Then he told me that the world
is not as it appears to be frontward, not then, not now, and to
leave the world, to see the power of the spirit on the hills, we
had to walk out of the known world backward.

"We had to walk backward so no one would follow us up
the hill, and my father said that things that follow are things that
demand attention," said Belladonna. "Do you think we are being
followed now?"

"No, not at night," said Bishop Parasimo.

"When I do this, we are walking and talking into the morning with Old Winter Catcher, walking and talking backward down the road," she said. "We are the first to come into morning with no demands on our attention, and noitnetta ruo no sdnamed on htiw gninrom otni emoc ot tsrif eht."

Shaman High University smelled of wildflowers and bears and landfill refuse when the teaching trickster ended his crossblood stories. Clement Beaulieu soared backward out the window in the darkness and laughed ha ha ha haaaa over the mountains and familiar tribal faces on the water moons.

Interstate Reservation

MONSIGNOR Lusitania Missalwait was late for the last episode in his luminous roadside war stories. Someone had locked the stout old man in an outhouse and borrowed his motorcycle. Never undone, and determined to buoy his blood in white water, he pried loose the seat cover, brushed aside webs and dead flies, sloshed out the back, and marched the whole distance from the treeline to his concrete interstate in the dark.

The clerical title of honor was not an altar commission, but he does, believe it or not, own a section of interstate highway with one bridge and an exit to a small town near the White Earth Reservation in Minnesota.

He was born on the reservation, May 7, 1915, the same day the steamship *Lusitania* was torpedoed and sunk near the Irish coast. His mother was a word griever and a shaman who routed bedimmed souls and cornered wicked shadows. She held birds near her ears when she listened to men, and she healed small animals, children, and women drunkards, in that order. His father was a reservation grunter, unnamed in an oral tradition; a white woodcutter who licked a frozen bit and lost his alien tongue on the same night his last son was born and the steamer was torpedoed.

"Now, the first picture on the screen, you see, that there is where Monsignor Lusitania Missalwait was conceived," said Supine Summer, the urban war stories projectionist. Soupie, as she is known on the reservation, was the last in her families to serve tribal men and bear the names of the seasons.

The transparencies, like her surnames, dissolved on four wide screens suspended over the interstate lanes in both directions. The steamer rises, prow and funnels above the wake, and birch bark scrolls, loose plastic windows, wither in black and white. Horses hold at the pales. The peevish wind moans on the barbed wire near the shoulder.

"Shadows are thin in the cities, darker where the shamans wait," she chanted. "He brought the urban wars back home to the reservation in a sidecar, on bald tires, with this motorcycle, the one in this picture here."

Monsignor Missalwait wore a surplice on the first screen; the loose vestments dissolved and the old crossblood appeared in a chicken feather headdress. On the second screen a blonde issued from the sidecar, her hair back on the wind, but she faded when a thundercloud shrouded the pond near the mission on-screen. The third and fourth screens transmuted the faces of tribal children to wild blooms.

Summer kneaded the microphone in the narrow barter booth on the median. When she smiled her mouth turned down. The huge loudspeakers shivered and her voice boomed ten miles down the road, over the peneplain. "Watch your speed out there, and remember at the end of the week there is a celebration because my name changes with the season, and now, a march to the war stories."

Four trucks and two sedans were double parked on the rough shoulder. From the mound behind the barter booth, whole families watched the feral black and white urban battle scenes dissolve on the screens. The pictures were shot low, knee high in concrete, fast foods, and broken rails. Bodies wobbled and fingers drummed in time to *The National Fencibles* and *Semper Fidelis* by John Philip Sousa. The sound track hissed, harsh snares, and a paradiddle rushed over the piccolos. Mongrels barked, but their voices were lost in the march.

Minnesota, like other states on the winter rim, nurtures those wild characters who weave their blood with the seasons and who mend the seams between cold crows and withered trees, warm hands and barbed leaves, golden peaches, pinch bean schemes, and the laughter of children in the cedar. Missalwait resolved to heal ten miles of the linear world with his urban war stories. Supine holds his light and sound on that wild tribal road.

The Federal Highway Commission, in accordance with federal policies to decentralize certain public services, offered sections of interstate highways for sale to the highest bidders. The new enterprise received state and federal subsidies for section maintenance of up to ten miles, and each entrepreneur was awarded special shares in coin operated rest stop ventures. The new endowments, according to press releases, would encourage imaginative management practices and reduce federal costs. These ten-mile interstate endowments were made in heaven for tricksters on the move.

Monsignor Missalwait never couched an interstate interest, and he had no cash or patent land to bid; he had little more than his blood and the urban war stories he told in fair weather at a natural amphitheater behind his cabin on the reservation.

Supine Autumn, who was a bank teller at the time, told the old crossblood that he could bid his blood for a slice of the interstate. "The government," she said, "will provide investment loans to minorities."

"Minorities?"

"Chicken feathers."

"White meat?"

"Reservation minorities," she said and then explained the provisions, prepared his application, and before her name turned to Spring he became the proud owner of ten miles of interstate.

Monsignor Missalwait wore his beaded surplice for the ownership ceremonies. Two federal officials were situated at the north end of the section. The interstate trust treaties were embossed with an oversized chop and bound with red plastic. The officials practiced their smiles, signed for the president and various government secretaries, holstered their pens, folded their ceremonial table, and turned back toward the capital.

"One buck to pass," said Missalwait.

"For what?"

"Turned the table on the great father."

"The president is not amused."

"Fine on the president."

"The president is never fined."

"The president is fined one buck to remove blankets from our reservation over this interstate, which is now mine," said the old crossblood with his hands laced beneath the surplice. He rocked on his heels and watched the crows circle the government sedan while he explained in pious tones that his section was located on sovereign tribal land.

Spring erected barriers and then, in minutes, she unloaded two fish houses to serve as toll booths, one at each end of the interstate section. The signs explained that the ten-mile toll could be paid in cash or barter. The first receipt was issued to the great white father for one blanket.

Monsignor Missalwait tottered at the end of the march into

the narrow barter booth. Breathless, he wiped his brow and stout neck. Summer smiled and then she pinched her nose while he explained what had happened at the outhouse. His black trousers were wet with excrement. His nostrils flared when he leaned over the microphone and concluded his series of urban war stories.

"In the beginning," he began, "we were stones that rolled down the mountains and gathered in piles here and there as we are now in cities and towns, but some stones rolled back and became tricksters."

Summer collected cash and barter from those who had arrived late to hear the stories and then she moved back from the booth, but the stench on the old crossblood followed her in the dark. She waited in the shadows, and when he touched his ears, the signal to begin, she started the last recorded tape of his urban war stories and projected urban scenes on four screens. His voice battered the humid interstate, words mustered on metal, in the blood, on the crown, hands, ornaments, four bright screens:

"The San Francisco Sun Dancers got hooked on their urban illusions of the past and never rolled back. Listen to their drum music, the sound is down and oppressive. Their clothes are dark, black hats, black shirts, cosmetic boots, solemn and sullen transmuted frowns. There are no trickeries in them to heal at the western drum. The beat is too dark to turn a smile in the cities. Their primal sound downs birds, hauls winter to the new gardens in the window."

Summer turned down the volume.

Missalwait pinched his nose and listened to his own voice with the dance on four screens. "Indian inventions are so compelling that thousands of white people, lost and separated like their children who are pictured on milk cartons, spill out their new tribal identities each night on television talk shows, take to chicken feathers, descriptive names, and dance in isolated circles on the concrete with burnished cheeks.

"Anaïs Nin wrote about the tribal inventions that wander in the cities, on a 'slow walk like a somnambulist enmeshed in the past and unable to walk into the present.' She saw the noble invention alone on the streets, 'loaded with memories, cast down by them,' and she wrote that 'he saw only the madness of the world.'"

"Nin never owned an interstate," mocked Summer.

"She never waded in shit to quote me either," said the crossblood. He wrinkled his nose, removed his trousers, and pitched them over the barbed wire at the shoulder of the road.

"The Indians who spurn the inventions become invisible, imperfect victims with common names. Those who boarded the colonial transition trains became proud planners and tribal merchants who shipped their new inventions back to the reservations. Nothing is secure now but silence and secrets."

Summer smirked and covered her ears.

Someone honked a horn.

Urban tribes appeared on the four screens.

Missalwait boomed, "Doc Cloud Burst, creator of the San Francisco Sun Dancers, keeper of urban tribal traditions, and dispenser of downtown descriptive dream names, cupped his enormous ear in the tribal manner, whipped the faces on the drum, down down down down, and wailed in cultural pain."

Cloud Burst appeared on the first screen in the back seat of a black limousine. The seats were beaded, and feathers decorated the window frames. He was pictured outside various fast food restaurants and at selected parks.

His six disciples—Bad Mouth and her brother Knee High,

Fast Food, Touch Tone, Injun Time, Fine Print—and one white-skin, Token White, responded to his beck at the drum with frowns and expressions of profound cultural torment.

Urban scenes at docks and parks continued on the fourth screen, while the disciples appeared on the second and third screens over the interstate. Token White carried a bow and arrows.

"Those drum clowns live for foul weather times four," said Professor Peter Rosebed on-screen, otherwise known in more intimate circles as the Pink Stallion because he was a crossblood, neither red nor white. "To them humor and kindness are forms of punishment, like urban contraries, or puritanical. Their fractured visions and illusions of power come from fast food, thunder, and the roar of traffic on the interstates."

"Witnesses or survivors?" the old crossblood mocked his own recorded interstate show. He leaned back, balanced on an aluminum chair behind the barter booth.

"Confessors?" asked Summer.

"You might ask if these urban tribes are witnesses or survivors. The answer is neither, there is no trace of personal experience, their lives are borrowed from the past.

"Their lives are material, the blues died on their western drums. All of them, right down to the last plastic bear claw and false braid, would rather be blonde," said the Pink Stallion. He celebrated tribal ironies, and he never missed a moment in praise of blondes.

"Darkness, total miasmal beats, for sure," he said with obvious pleasure in his choice of words. Rosebed had studied mythic structures and the oral tradition, but he boasted carnal encounters rather than theoretical interruptions.

"Listen, dark skin is not the darkness."

"Nor is fair skin an illumination," said Summer. The new

stories she edited, the selection of transparencies, and the events at the barter booth were more interesting than her studies at college and her duties at the bank. "These three voice dramas are the best, and you even pay me more than the bankers."

"These poor urban savages are the perfect hosts for failure and cultural contradictions," announced Monsignor Missalwait. The loudspeakers hissed and then clicked several times. The crossblood had tapped the microphone with his ring during the recording.

Rosebed was standing under the sycamores on-screen when a tall blonde, known as the nude dance advocate, danced like a sunbeam over the dark thunder at the western drum, and as she danced she removed her blouse and flashed her small firm white breasts.

"What the hell are you doing in there?" a woman asked. Her voice boomed over the loudspeakers; she repeated the question, and then an engine roared. Missalwait had forgotten to stop the tape recorder when the car approached the barrier; the conversation from the barter booth was broadcast as part of the urban war stories.

"One dollar," answered Monsignor Missalwait.

"Don't have a dollar."

"What do you have?"

"Nothing," said the woman.

"Come to the stories then," he said.

"What stories?"

"Free urban war stories."

"When?"

"Sunday night with pictures."

"God willing," she said with a salute and roared past the booth when he raised the barrier. She honked and blinked the lights when she heard the recorded conversation that night.

Cloud Burst whipped the faces on the dream drum harder, thundered hard, and raised his voice to a pitched pain. Small leaves trembled on the trees. Between wails, he motioned with his thin lips, in the tribal manner, toward his disciples. Token White nodded back from the drum circle. She protected her drum father and moved toward the blonde with the little breasts.

Token White, tall, thin, angular, with an unattractive gait and a downward curl to her lower lip, was the one blonde member of the San Francisco Sun Dancers. She danced for father sun, her special burden, and bore his dream name. Born on a corn farm, she came to urban studies on a scholarship but double-crossed the academic world with terminal creeds.

White became a master archer, an expert on bows and arrows, and turned tribal in place of books and theories. She embodied total racial, spiritual, and cultural opposition behind the bow, an archer at war with civilization and technologies. White hates her color and shape in the world, and she shares this hatred with the urban tribes who hate whites, a perfect match.

Token White lumbered over to the nude dance advocate and drew her bow with a black arrow. She followed as the dancer rolled her shoulders and breasts in sensual semicircles. The drum thundered at the side.

"Classic, this is a classic scene," raved the Pink Stallion in the thunder and sunshine on-screen. "This is the perfect demonstration of double cultural contradictions. Those two should cancel each other out, like double negatives. Two blondes, one a token in opposition to the other with the same reasons."

"What was that?" asked Summer.

"Blondes are in perfect opposition to the invented tribes, but pardon me for loving blondes, and nude dance advocates, more than throwback archers in black hats."

"Do you know this person?" asked Summer.

"Too much oral tradition," answered Missalwait.

"Behind the tribal counter."

"Token White uses tribal culture like a prescription for a headache," said Rosebed. "Look at her there, built like a crooked limb, crude like a bad bow, while the blonde dancer moves through culture from the inside, her side, our side, not the outside, not a deprivation model for culture, not a mere concept for being alive. She is alive.

"The urban tribes have it all turned around, too much tradition on the mind and not enough heart in the crotch," Rosebed said with his hands on his crotch. "Prescription cultures bind them in time, too much owned from the past tenses. Dreams and the inside are closed down for repairs, not enough celebration light and real flesh.

"Listen, blondes are wonderful, but tribal cultures and blondes are like bad doctors for the soul," he said, and his wild hands cut each word to size.

"Listen, white bitch, our dream drum music is sacred," snapped Token White to the blonde dancer who cupped her breasts and shimmered once more over the thunder and the pain of the drumbeat.

"Monsignor Lusitania Missalwait, is that the name of a real priest?" asked a man at the barrier. He leaned out the window closer to the barter booth to hear, unaware that his voice was recorded with the last episode of the urban war stories.

"That is my whole name," said the crossblood.

"The province or the liner?"

"What does he mean by that?" asked Summer.

"The liner," he told the man at the barrier.

"Portugal was once named Lusitania," he explained to Summer.

"Why not for the nation then?" she asked.

"Named for the dead?" asked the recorded voice.

"Mother Missalwait was a griever," said the old crossblood. "She set the world right with words, like a table, but it was never the same from meal to meal, tree to tree, season to season, because she believed that what ended by chance was never dead but waited for a time to be discovered in dreams and names. So, the steamer returned with me one night, nine months from a wild conception over wild rice in a rented canoe."

"When were you ordained?"

"Let me answer that," she said. Summer leaped from her aluminum chair and waded like a heron around the barter booth. "The mission priest said he was real touched. He said he could patch leaks better than any halfbreed he ever knew on the reservation, but that was nothing to remember when he started his stories about the urban tribes in the cedar theater out back."

"August 12, 1970."

"Lusitania heals birds like his mother, but he never liked drunkards," Summer continued between recorded voices. The scenes dissolved with the conversations, and somehow the narrative made sense; more than a dozen families stopped on the shoulder to watch and listen. "Then we discovered that when he was at the natural theater behind his cabin there were no flies or mosquitoes there, and when the thunder boomed all around it never rained when he was there. He was ordained by nature, in the cedar, and all the crossbloods agreed."

"*Dominus vobiscum*," chanted Missalwait.

"Would you like to sell your interstate?" the man asked.

"Never, never. How much?"

"Never, is right," said Summer.

"Does it rain here?" asked the recorded voice.

"Not on the barter booth."

"But tell me, are you a real Indian?"

"Partial invention."

"This is an honoring song, bitch," Token White hissed through her clenched teeth on-screen. "No bare tits allowed, so move out before we honor your ass with an arrow."

Cloud Burst waited for her to return during the last night of her urban vision search. The other members of the San Francisco Sun Dance all started for their four night vision in the same urban place and returned on time to meet father sun in the morning.

Token White started at Union Square with no money, no food, and the same instructions as the others to seek an urban vision on the streets. She was the first whiteskin to be initiated, and now she was late for her dream name ceremonial.

Each disciple received the same sacred instructions to return to the old traditions in mind and heart, speak to the four directions and to four people on the streets—an old man who remembers the past, mother earth, and her two children, the sun and water spirits. The visioneers were told to live on the streets, in dumpsters but not hotel lobbies, for four nights in search of a personal spiritual guardian and then to walk across the Golden Gate Bridge to the ceremonial bunker at Fort Cronkite, near Rodeo Lagoon.

The disciples were pierced on the breasts with plastic skewers fastened to leather laces bound to the sacred cottonwood tree at the ceremonial bunker. The disciples faced the rising sun, their father, and danced in circles on mother earth until a dream name was called out for the first time.

Cloud Burst told his sacred dancers that he learned in a dream that Token White would be late. He had a similar dream when Injun Time was late, but because it rained that morning, father sun was also late, so Fine Print saved the day when he raised a new father sun made from orange aluminum foil on a broom handle. Since then, and because the weather is seldom clear in the morning over the ceremonial bunker, the San Francisco Sun Dancers raise and lower their own sun in their own sacred time.

Token White drew her Navaho bow three hours before dawn on the fourth night and threw four flaming reed arrows over the ceremonial bunker from the four directions. The sinew hummed with each arrow.

Cloud Burst said the flaming arrows were all according to his dream. The disciples saw the arrows as a sacred message from the great spirit. Then Token White threw a padded arrow with a note attached into the bunker. A message was printed on plain brown paper. Cloud Burst, who could not read, passed the note to Fine Print, who cleared his throat and then imitated the halting voice of his spiritual leader as he read:

> Father Cloud Burst
> you sure did trust me to be a disciple
> and my heart pounded like a medicine drum.
> But because my skin is white
> my shadow is white too,
> which makes me feel ashamed father.
> I am over the hill now,
> but if you want me call me from the four directions
> then I will come to be pierced
> and never return to my white shadow again.

Fine Print cleared his throat at the end of the message. The ceremonial bunker was silent. Ocean waves lapped over the rocks on the shore. The air was moist and cold, too cold to bare a chest. The disciples waited for their leader to instruct them.

Cloud Burst motioned with his hands and head in the four

directions, to the stars and moon, rubbed his face and bare chest with smoke from the cedar fire, and then began to wail in a low voice. He wailed until he slipped through his own shadow in a vision, and then he pierced his chest muscles with plastic skewers once more, in the same old scars, for the sacred sun dance. He leaned back, danced in a slow circle, and pulled the leather laces tight from the cottonwood tree in the center of the bunker. Fine Print danced on the other side of the tree with his father.

Cloud Burst raised his arms, pulled back hard on the leather laces until his flesh ripped open, the cottonwood tree shuddered in place, and he called her dream name for the first time in the four sacred directions.

"Token White," he called to the north on-screen.

"Token White," Summer called to the west in the booth.

"Token White," he called to the south.

"Token White," the families on the shoulder called to the east. Horns honked and lights blinked in celebration. The disciples appeared on the four screens, poised around a cedar fire like lost animals.

"Token White, come home to your father, come home now, come home, give yourself to father sun, come home to the bunker and be a proud urban tribal warrior with white skin." The voice of the urban sun dancer boomed in the darkness.

"Come home to the barter booth," mocked Summer.

"Here I come," said Token White. Tears bounced down her low angular cheekbones. She lumbered over the mound through the succulent plants with her bow and arrows, the new urban warrior with a vision of an invented tribal past.

Cloud Burst, her new father with the sun, took her in his arms near the cottonwood tree. The warm blood on his chest spread on her breasts. He moved back and opened her flannel shirt near the fire. Steam rose from her dark wide nipples. He pierced her hard breasts with the same plastic skewers that cut his flesh, for the ceremonial erection of her new father sun.

Token White danced in hundreds of circles, tireless, each new move a wonderful dream world, around and around the cottonwood tree, she would not break. Fine Print tired; the foil sun on the pole leaned low on the horizon of the bunker. Cloud Burst put his arms around her from behind, cupped her breasts, and then leaned backward with her and pulled the skewers from her breasts. He turned her around, and while she wailed he sucked the blood from her nipples and then spread her warm blood on his forehead and cheeks. The other disciples copied their master.

"Urban savages," someone called from the darkness on the interstate when the four screens pictured her breasts and the cheeks of the disciples covered with blood.

"We want our money back," a woman shouted.

"The war stories are free," said Missalwait.

"Never mind," said Summer.

Token White braced her short curved Apache bow, made from a white hickory wheel hoop, drew a hazelwood arrow with trimmed woodpecker feathers and a hand flaked obsidian point, the one she learned how to make in the mountains, and aimed it at the bare breasted dancer.

The nude blonde faced the sun at noon. She rolled her head and shoulders several times before she noticed the archer crouched behind the pruned trees at the rim of the campus plaza. She rolled to the sun once more, shivered in the face of violence, and then covered her breasts and moved into the crowd. The blonde smiled from a distance and became a passive white witness to an urban tribal dance.

"Shit, man, these white blondes are sick, sick, sick, sick," Bad Mouth screamed from the pruned sycamores. Knee High repeated each of her words, a whispered echo like a puppet at her side.

"First the blondes are boiled in hate, then comes cultural genocide, academic white tape, and then she bedews colonialism with her extreme spittle," said Rosebed. "Bad Mouth has a terminal case of colonial throat."

"Colonial throat?" asked Summer.

"The real colonist is a crazed blonde caught at the back of her throat," said Rosebed. His laughter was too loud to share the humor of the obscene gestures that followed his description on-screen.

"Deep throat," someone chanted from the shoulder.

"Never mind," said Summer. She rushed to the barter booth and turned the volume higher on the recorder to override the voices of the chanters in the trucks near the second screen on the interstate.

Token White lowered her bow and returned the arrow to her beaded otter skin quiver. She sat in the sacred circle of thunder at the western drum.

"More tits and less drums," a voice demanded.

"No drums," said Summer.

"Forgive me father sun," said Token White. She once confessed her romantic discoveries of tribal people at a summer seminar on child development. When she was thirteen, tall and unattractive for her age, she discovered Indians in the book *Ishi in Two Worlds*, by Theodora Kroeber. Token told how Ishi became her best friend for at least two years, until Doc Cloud Burst called her dream name in the four directions at the bunker.

Ishi taught her how to use a bow and arrow to hunt food in the wooded mountains near Mount Lassen. Token said she was caught with Ishi, the last two survivors of the Yahi tribe; she confessed that she was taken with Ishi to live in the Museum of Anthropology at the University of California.

"It was late in the season," she told the students that summer, "in the morning, near a slaughterhouse, when the two of us were cornered by dogs against a corral fence. We were brave, and I told Ishi the things the sheriff said when we were locked up in cells, because he could not speak our language. We were tired and hungry. Then all sorts of skins came to our cell, talking in all different languages, and we understood what the skins said but we did not answer because the whites were listening.

"The sheriff showed us the headlines about us in the newspapers. We were wild Indians, and I was embarrassed, but the stories helped us to meet some good white people. We got to know some anthropologists, and we liked them too, Alfred Kroeber and Thomas Waterman. And then there was a medical doctor, Saxton Pope, he was an archer and we liked him the best. Very important people.

"Ishi and Doctor Pope taught me all that I know about bows and arrows and hunting. We hated crowds, and when the museum opened, Phoebe Apperson Hearst, and Benjamin Ide Wheeler, he was the president of the University of California then, and other important people came to look at us in the museum like we were freaks or something in a circus," she said and looked past Sather Tower to Strawberry Creek Canyon.

"It hurts me to tell you this," said Token. "Ishi started to cough in the museum, he seemed tired, he gained too much weight, we both did when we were captured, and he died in the spring. Doctor Pope was there. Ishi smiled at both of us before he started walking backwards into the next world.

"Ishi said, 'ne ma yahi . . . wahle injin,' which meant, 'are you an indian, a valley indian,'" said Token White. "He also said 'kopee' for coffee, and I loved him more than anyone else in the whole wide world," she said, tears running down her cheeks, "until I met Doc Cloud Burst, now he is my father. When Ishi died I turned back to the mountains to be alone and wild, and it was there that I learned more about bows and arrows."

Pink Stallion asked her what she did in the mountains, and she said that she had been an eagle and a bear and an otter, in that order, and once "I was even a wild mountain stream running down through the redwoods to the sea."

"You dumped that to dance around a western drum?" asked Rosebed with one finger on his nose. She was nervous from the dance, and her dense armpits had an acrid odor.

"Streams were not enough," answered Token White.

"Neither are bears," said Summer.

"Show me your bows," said the Pink Stallion.

"Not a chance," answered Summer.

"Do you know about bows?" she asked and then handed him several. Rosebed touched the wood and strummed the sinew. She told him how to throw an arrow and how to make points from obsidian. When she spoke she drew civilization into the wilderness, into the mountains and down the streams in her imagination and memories.

The first bow was a short bow, her "sacred bow," she said, a Yahi bow, "the bow Ishi taught me to make from a single piece of mountain juniper." She braced the bow and pointed out the natural deer sinew string and the graceful oval curve of the limbs. The string snapped and hummed with a "sweet tune," she said, and then she explained what that meant.

"Sweet must be sweet," mocked Pink Stallion.

"Sweet to the archer means well balanced," she said and then explained that the arrows were made from hazel sticks and rolled over heated stones to make them smooth. "Ishi taught me how to make smooth arrows."

The arrows had four feathers, trimmed feathers for a better spin in flight. White pointed out that "Ishi used three feathers, one bird wing for each arrow."

Doctor Saxton Pope taught her how to make the other bows. She told two more stories, however, before she presented the other bows. One was about riding on horseback with Doctor Pope and Ishi back to the mountains to live in the old way. "Ishi called animals in the sacred manner of a hunter, he had a sweet voice."

The second event she told about was the time she went swimming in the nude in Deer Creek with Ishi and Doctor Pope and his son. Token was embarrassed when she told these stories; she seemed concerned about what people might think.

She told stories from visual memories, from the oral tradition; she was there in the places she described. Rosebed pretended to be there, he smiled when he saw her in the nude. She was embarrassed for her wide nipples and the angular shape of her body.

"More, more, more than blood," several voices chanted on the median of the interstate as she appeared on the first and second screens. The scenes dissolved when she turned toward the camera.

The Mohave bow, she told the Pink Stallion, is made from a single stave of willow, smoked in cedar to temper the wood. The bark from the limb was still on the back of the bow. Holding the bow, she explained that "this bow is better in the morning when it is cool, because the wood is harsh in warm temperatures."

"My bones too," said Summer.

"This is my sweetest bow, it hums with a fine balance," said Token. The Navaho bow was made from mesquite wood with a buckskin bound handgrip. She had used the Navaho bow to throw four flaming arrows over the ceremonial bunker.

The last bow in her collection was the Apache bow, the one made from a white hickory wagon hoop, which she had used to draw an arrow on the nude dancer. "This is my cupid bow, because it has a wheel curve to the limbs."

Pink Stallion stroked the curve and snickered.

Cloud Burst reset his black wide brimmed hat, whipped the same old faces on the drum one last time, and ended the honoring music for students on campus on-screen over the interstate. The other drummers knew when to stop; they raised their wands like shorebirds, beaks high near the ocean waves, and the beat ended on shore. The urban tribes drum and summon the thunder to know the silence.

"So ends the first series of urban war stories," said Monsignor Missalwait. His stolen motorcycle was the last picture to dissolve on the four screens over the sovereign interstate. He thought he heard the engine in the distance.

"Autumn is my birthday next week," said Summer.

"Remember Soupie," said Missalwait.

"No tolls on my birthday."

"Listen, whoever borrowed my motorcycle, would you please return it now?" the crossblood pleaded over the loudspeakers. "We might have to run curious blondes to the cedar theater for a screen test with their bows and arrows, mea culpa, mea culpa."

The Psychotaxidermist

Colonel Clement Beaulieu leaned into the autumn with his trickster stories. The old crossblood was the last to remember the fur trader, and near the end of his adventures he walked down the hard earth trail three times a week to the Saint Benedict Catholic Mission on the White Earth Reservation.

He trailed three black mongrels and turned over in his mind the stories and stones he would remember with the old priests and nuns that night at dinner. His white hair sailed on the wind, the best season of his time.

Colonel Clement smiled over his uncommon memories. The wrinkles and winter tracks on his thin face opened with interior humors. The rave mongrels pitched their heads back, tongues swerved to the side, when he cleared his throat four times and gestured with his lips in the tribal manner. The throat, he said, "must be prepared to tell trickster stories," and so he imagined an oral tradition four sounds ahead of the printed word.

"District Court Judge Silas Bandied snapped his ceramic teeth in the hollow downtown courtroom," Colonel Clement said to the mongrels on the road to the mission. He remembered the strange stories about the first psychotaxidermist, the tribal shaman of dead animals. "The judge cleared his throat three times, his ceremonial trine, a cormorant at the breakwater, and then he read the sentence:

" 'Shaman Newcrows, alias Random New Crows, alias The Crow, alias The Psychotaxidermist, we have reviewed the charges and the best evidence here and find you this fine morning full of guilt without a doubt,' said the judge. 'This court sentences you now and forever to serve ten years at hard labor for the crime of wild animule molestation, and indecent liberties with dead animules in public places, to wit, a golf course, the first in the state, might we add here, and then . . .' "

"Evidence?" questioned Newcrows.

"Silence," commanded Bandied. "The evidence is clear that you were dressed in a bear animule mask, rapacious sight that it must have been that night, and . . ."

"Ceremonial bear," insisted Newcrows, who was leaning back in his chair at a comfortable escape distance from the judge and the prosecutor. He was dressed in a red velvet suit with a bear claw necklace. Newcrows was a hummer; he sounded human, but his head waved from side to side, the morning motion of the bear in him, and his distance, his powerful energies danced through the memories of oak and cedar and summer ponds on the wild rim of the courtroom.

"Nothing more than a circus bear mask, leaning over dead animules at the golf course, which you admitted stuffing."

"Take care with what you say out loud here," warned Newcrows. "The animals and birds are sure to have their way with your memories."

"Rubbish," sneered the judge. "Dead is dead, and no man, not to mention you and your animules, has ever come back from the dead. No sane man that is."

"What dead animals?"

"Indian evildoer," said the judge. He pointed and snapped his teeth over the bench. "Savage, how dare you defile this courtroom with your word trickeries? You are pitiable, beyond contempt, and must remain silent in my courtroom mister savage."

"Your Honor, please," pleaded the prosecutor, whose face and neck were covered with brown tick bites, "please consider this; we dropped the charges on this man because we lost the dead evidence."

"You lost the dead animules?"

"Yes, Your Honor," responded the narrow prosecutor. He scratched the bites on his chest and arms. "We had the dead evidence on the fourth green, but it up and disappeared during a thunderstorm."

"Mister Prosecutor," said the judge with his thin cormorant neck over his dark bench, "let me warn you now. This crime took place on our new golf course, and this is no time for you to misplace the evidence, dead or alive. We will recess a few minutes now for you to gather your wits and find the dead evidence to convict this man."

Judge Bandied was a charter member of the new golf course at the Town and Country Club of Saint Paul. "I was the one who dropped the first official putt with a green ball," he boasted, "through the snow and cold on February 11, 1888, when the course first opened." Now, during the first full season, the fourth hole had been fouled forever, so the judge reasoned, and that because of "some strange dead animule exorcism by a damned circus clown in a bear mask."

Shaman Newcrows was born on the shores of Bad Medicine Lake on the White Earth Reservation and blessed with animal spirits and avian visions. He traveled in magical flight, he said, through "four levels of consciousness and the underworld." During the summer when he was twelve, lightning flashed from the eyes of seven crows in his dreams. He took his spirit name from the crows, and from bears, the ursine shivers in the night, and he took from the woods for the first time the languages of animals and birds and flowers and trees. Since then he has listened to animals, trees, earth, and the west wind.

Newcrows heard the wise crows curse the evil in humans; that much could have been traditional, but the caws in his world were missions. His vision revealed that crows lusted for tribal women, their pleasures in tone and color, and their raucous conversations, crow to crow in the white birch, were seldom more than sexual rumors.

Newcrows heard his own voice rumble from the heart of a bear. He waited down at the treeline near the water, slow and certain in his manner and motion; he laughed once at his solitude, and at darkness, the warm interior of his sacred maw. He heard the words of the bears, and he heard animal languages that humans were once able to understand.

Newcrows saw in his vision, from the lightning that flashed around him, the auras and shadows of trees towering over their sacred stumps. The cedar and white pine spirits spoke to him from their ancient places on the earth, from the places where trees were cut, down but not dead, and the stumps recited the names of the cutters and the places in the cities where their bodies were sold as beams and fence posts. He worried as a child and tried to return loose boards to the trees.

Newcrows listened to the animals and trees; they told him that the dead would return to the earth. Under a new moon, said an otter, his brothers and sisters would return in face and breath from the land of the dead. The trees told about the coming fires when their ashes would return to the earth with their woodland memories.

Newcrows dreamed that strokes of lightning would resurrect all dead animals and those who praised and celebrated their lives. Whenever he passed beneath a tree, or watched a bird in flight, wolves on the run, beaver, insects turning in the morning sun, the crows in their stories, he heard them whisper the words that would return them to the earth. In his vision he was told by the animals to deliver their dead to the great spirit, and to do so during a thunderstorm.

Newcrows, on the outside, was neither tree nor otter; in his manner he was three parts fool with most humans. His head rolled on the run, and he dropped words in simple phrases, lost his references to time; and the colonial agents on the reservation solicited his signature, his precious mark, five times for federal treaties with the tired tribes because he could remember but one line at one place at one time. His memories were episodic, and he did not understand the world in grammars, models, cumulatives, plurals, or generalizations.

When he was three years old he walked into the woods alone as his mother gathered wild rice. He was lost for three days, and his mother feared the spirits had taken him to the underworld, but then on the morning of the fourth day he walked out of the woods with a wide smile, with bear hair on his face and clothes.

Newcrows was silent for nine years; he heard the world in his visions with animals and trees until he was twelve. He tossed his head, trailed the bears in the woods, laughed and shivered with the trees and mongrels, and never worried about speech, or thought about possessions until he saw a naked woman.

"Stop drooling and open the door," said Sister Isolde to the peeping stranger she saw stuck between the logs. Her white breasts wambled in the light from the fire.

Newcrows blinked twice and turned to the darkness. He

ran, but before he disappeared, she rushed through the door and stopped him at the treeline.

Sister Isolde lived with several mongrels and a loyal fox in a small cabin she had built from scraps; the cabin was located near Mallard, an abandoned sawmill town on the White Earth Reservation. Little remained of the town but her cabin and huge piles of sawdust. She was abandoned, too, at age ten, the lonesome daughter of a skidder and a timbertown prostitute.

Newcrows cawed over her body and laughed too much with the animals that night; the fox snapped at his bare feet and chased him back to the woods with the bears in the morning. Months later he remembered his vision to return the dead animals to the earth.

Newcrows collected the dead from natural and unnatural causes and waited for lightning and the great storm. He perched and posed thousands of birds and animals near the shore of Bad Medicine Lake. The animals decomposed and were carried away by millions of flies, not lightning. Not one bird or animal came back to the earth. The fetid odor burned in the nostrils of the tribe, but it was not that or his familial nonfluencies that led to his removal; the white government agents ordered him to leave the reservation. He was banished at last from the one place on the earth where he remembered the earth.

Newcrows traveled from reservation to reservation and gathered dead animals. The word was out about his strange habits, and he was asked to leave, leave, leave. He sought the secret of preserving the dead, not knowing how long the dead should wait for the lightning storm. He asked white people. A mortician taught him the art of taxidermy, but stuffing animals transformed their images and separated their bones and blood from their spirit, and that with no ceremonies. He listened to tribal prophets and urban tricksters speak of new spirits and resurrections; their realities were tied to words, but not names.

He learned how to hold the dead for the storm from a woman who lived at La Pointe on Madeline Island in Lake Superior. She lived near a cemetery and talked to the dead at night. She taught him to imagine the dead, and the dead told him stories. He gathered the dead, tied their bones, and waited for the storm.

"Your Honor," pleaded the prosecutor as he scratched his neck and shoulders, "if it pleases the court, permit me to continue with my explanation."

"Mister prosecutor, remember this, our fourth hole has been defiled forever with these strange animules," Bandied warned, his neck extended over the oak bench. "We must not allow this terrible crime to pass without punishment, fitting punishment."

"Yes, Your Honor," said the prosecutor. "Now, permit me this review. We found the accused, the man here in court named New Crows . . ."

"Newcrows."

"What?"

"Newcrows, one word, one consciousness, one time in all to live on the earth as a bird and animal," shouted Newcrows.

"New Crows, we found Newcrows on the fourth hole under a full moon dressed in a bear costume and dancing around hundreds of dead birds and animals which he explained were his friends. Now, we arrested him then and there, but because the evidence was so strange, we left it in situ and called the zoo. The animals were dead but somehow they appeared to be still living, and, forgive the contradictions, Your Honor, asleep, motionless, but with their eyes open, alert, awake, and poised, more like creatures waiting to attack or to be attacked. The experience was too strange to move, but before the zoo people could get there, a thunderstorm blew up from nowhere and when lightning struck all around the fourth green, the animals and birds let out this horrible primal scream, loud and clear, and then, sure as you see me here before you now, the dead evidence walked, some ran, loped, and leaped, and flew with the storm. Not even a feather or a claw remained on the fourth hole as evidence."

"Damn your evidence," wailed Bandied. "There must be evidence. Charge him with something as an evildoer then. Lock him up somehow."

"But we have no statute for evil."

"Psychotic and dangerous to the living, then," demanded Bandied, clearing his cormorant throat three times and stacking his stout white fingers on the bench.

"Dangerous to whom?"

"Not to whom."

"Dangerous to what then?"

"To the fourth green, to the human spirit," Bandied snapped again, "dangerous to civilization, men and women who take pleasure in outdoor exercise and a good game."

"But Your Honor."

"So, how did he do it?" asked the judge. He seemed more calm. "How did he do it with all those animals? What was the evil trick?"

"Never a trick," said Newcrows.

"Close your evil mouth in my courtroom," snapped the judge. His mood changed for the worse. "The accused is not permitted to speak to me. No telling what evil might come from your mouth."

"My words are from the dead," said Newcrows.

"Silence," demanded Bandied.

"Silence," mocked Newcrows.

"Silence that evildoer."

"Silence that evildoer."

"Officer, remove him now."

"Officer, remove me now."

"Prosecutor, please continue," said the judge.

"Your Honor, there is no more."

"How does he do it, fool?"

"Yes, yes, Your Honor, if it pleases the court, we have a letter from Samuel Mitchell, a medical doctor, to one Samuel Burnside, which was published in a recent edition of a book entitled *Study of Mortuary Customs Among the North American Indians* by H. C. Yarrow. This letter bears on your question, Your Honor, in that the letter and the female described in the letter are both held in the American Antiquarian Society.

"Mitchell writes, after examining a female corpse, that 'it is a human body found in one of the limestone caverns of Kentucky. . . . The skin, bones, and other firm parts are in a state of entire preservation. . . . The heart was in situ.' "

"What does that mean?" asked the judge.

"Your Honor, in situ means the pagans did not eat her heart out like they do the animals, or bears, for example," explained the prosecutor while he scratched harder at his chest and stomach.

"What is all this scratching?"

"Tribal ticks."

"What, if anything, can this evildoer know about bears or animules?" asked the judge. He leaned over behind his massive dark bench to scratch his ankles and did not hear the prosecutor read from *Bear Ceremonialism in the Northern Hemisphere*, a University of Pennsylvania dissertation written by A. Irving Hallowell:

" 'The categories of rational thought, by which we are ac-

customed to separate human life from animal life and the supernatural from the natural, are drawn upon lines which the
facts of primitive cultures do not fit.

" 'Animals are believed to have essentially the same sort of
animating agency which man possesses. They have a language
of their own, can understand what human beings say and do,
have forms of social or tribal organization, and live a life which
is parallel in other respects to that of human societies.

" 'Magical or supernatural powers are also at the disposal of
certain species; they may metamorphose themselves into other
creatures or, upon occasion, into human form. . . . Dreams may
become a specialized means of communication between man and
animals.' "

"Where did those ticks come from?" the judge asked as he
emerged from behind his bench. He pulled his black robe off and
scratched at his thighs and crotch.

"From the bears," explained the prosecutor, scratching at
his cheeks. "Bear ticks trained to disrupt our system of justice."

"That evildoer did this to us."

"Drop the charges," wailed the prosecutor while he scratched.
"Drop the goddamn charges and call the ticks off Your Honor."

"Charges dismissed!" screamed the judge from the floor behind his bench. He scratched and scratched like a reservation
mongrel on a tick mound. In seconds the bear ticks were gone
and the prosecutor and the judge were back at their benches and
chairs with their forms and robes and pencils and plurals.

Gathering his papers and charge sheets, the prosecutor
looked up at the judge and said: "Hallowell was told by an old
Indian that a bear . . ."

"Hollowill who?" asked Bandied.

"No, Your Honor, not Hollowill but Hallowell, the author
of *Bear Ceremonialism*, which we read into the record," explained

the prosecutor. "Hallowell was told by an old Indian that a bear is wiser than a man because a man does not know how to live all winter without eating anything."

Judge Bandied stretched his cormorant neck over his dark bench one more time and said, in a wild tone of voice, "But bears suck their paws and masturbate."

Colonel Clement rounded the last curve down the hill to Saint Benedict Mission. He pulled back his white hair, gestured to the mongrels with his lips in the tribal manner, cleared his throat four times, pushed the door open, and started his stories during the evening meal with the nuns and priests.

"This is a true tale from the reservation," Colonel Clement began, "about Sister Isolde, an old white shaman woman from Mallard who lived in an abandoned scapehouse that lightning struck four times each summer. The crows gossiped about her because she loved a bear who had a vision that he was human. Sister Isolde learned from the bear how to preserve the dead and how to train ticks to disrupt the evildoers in the white world.

"In Saint Paul, one summer before the turn of the century, when the first golf course was opened there, Sister Isolde followed her bear to the fourth green for a bear ceremonial with the dead, with thousands of dead birds and animals dancing under the full moon and waiting for the lightning to return them to the earth."

The mongrels pitched their heads back and waited outside for the stories to end on the inside. The mongrels waited for their master to lead them back through the dark before the storm. The animals were honored by his preparation.

Rattling Hail

RATTLING HAIL, he said in a harsh tone of voice, was his whole
name in all languages. He was a veteran from a recent war. For
his patriotic service as an enlisted man, representing the reservation prairie tribes, he was awarded several ribbons, which he
wore on the suit coat that he was given at a church, service connected dental care, educational benefits, and, for losing one leg
on a land mine, he was awarded a small pension as a disabled
veteran.

Clement Beaulieu, crossblood director of the American Indian Employment and Guidance Center when it was first opened
in Minneapolis, encountered Rattling Hail four times in four
months, as in a new urban ceremonial downtown on the reservation. On the first morning the center opened in a northside
settlement house, Rattling Hail appeared for the first time, hob-
bling across the hard tile floor on one crutch with one pant leg
tucked under his belt, folded and creased in a military manner.
Beaulieu was moving a desk when the decorated veteran halted
at the office door and stood at parade rest.

"Did you bastards open this place?"

"No, not the bastards."

"Who are you?" asked Rattling Hail.

"Beaulieu is the name," he said with a forced smile. "My people come from the White Earth Reservation. Who are you?"

"Remember Rattling Hail."

"Sacred name?" asked Beaulieu, referring to the tradition of giving sacred dream names to tribal children. The missionaries and government officials translated, with indifference to tribal cultures, familiar descriptive names and nicknames of tribal people as last names. Some missionaries thought that tribal descriptive names were sacred, but sacred names were seldom revealed to strangers.

In his book *The American Indian*, about tribal people on reservations at the turn of the last century, Warren Moorehead writes about the problem of familiar names entered on official tribal rolls. "Many years ago the employees at White Earth Agency made a roll of the Chippewa Indians. One would suppose that so important a document as a register of all the Indians would be accurate. But the original roll, as on file at the White Earth office, bristled with inaccuracies. For instance, the name Mah-geed is the Ojibwa pronunciation of Maggie. Many of the Indian girls were named Mah-geed by the priests and missionaries. Those who made the Government roll apparently thought that Mah-geed was a distinguished Indian name, so they had entered up quite a number of Mah-geeds. No other name is added.

"The Ojibwa name for old woman is Min-de-moi-yen. To the clerks who made the roll this sounded like the name of an Indian, so they solemnly set down many such names. Having assembled as our witnesses the most reliable old Indians, we were able to check up the many errors in the government roll. Frequently there would be as many as forty or fifty Ojibwa assembled in the schoolroom where our hearings were held. When the interpreter called out such a name as Min-de-moi-yen or

Mah-geed, the other Indians would shout with laughter, and, when they recovered sufficiently, they would state that they did not know what individual Indian was named as there were a score who might respond to that appellation."

"Rattling Hail," he said and waited at the door.

"Nickname a translation?" asked Beaulieu.

"Rattling Hail is Rattling Hail," he said, stressing over and over, with his lips drawn tight over his teeth, the word "hail." "Rattling Hail is the whole name, all the name. That sound is the world in me here, in all languages and tongues for all times. Remember Rattling Hail."

"Standing Rock in North Dakota?" asked Beaulieu. He was interested in locating his name on a reservation, the place for his name. Where one comes from is a cultural signature in the tribal world, a special sign, the casual diction of identities. Some reservations have had little contact with outsiders whereas others—the White Earth Reservation for example, about which Warren Moorehead wrote—have been virtual bicultural centers for intermarriage and cultural diffusion. Some reservations have crossblood roots to black and white, social and genetic evidence that black soldiers and white traders did more with the tribes than contain them in colonial exclaves. Crossbloods who hate white and black must hate that place and time in themselves.

"No reservation on me, no mixedblood should ask me about that," said Rattling Hail, grinding his teeth together. "What are you whitebloods doing here? What is this place?"

"We are setting up an employment and social services center, a new idea in urban centers for tribal people," explained Beaulieu. "You, believe it or not, are the first person through the door. We moved the desks in this morning."

"Whiteblood liars."

"Tell me about it," said Beaulieu.

"Bastard whites," he shouted. Rattling Hail raised his crutch and hobbled around the desk toward Beaulieu. His lips spread, like a cornered animal with no escape distance, exposing his clean, white, perfect teeth. "Check out the teeth," Beaulieu once told his friends, because perfect teeth in a tribal mouth means a government child, or dental care in a foster home. Most poor people have poor teeth to prove their past.

"Down with the crutch general," said Beaulieu as he moved around the room with the desk between them. "We opened the doors this morning, and here you are, the first one in the door. What is it you want here? Work, or some abusement?"

"Whiteblood liars," he said again and again as he hobbled around and around the desk, swinging the crutch. "No one ever helped us with nothing. Whiteblood liars."

"Now look, general, put down the crutch and walk out of here the same way you came in. This is not a good way to start anything," said Beaulieu. He stopped near the door to the office and waited. "This is no morning watering hole or abusement park, and no one needs you here to blame the world. Come back again when you are sober."

Rattling Hail lowered his crutch and hobbled toward the door. He stopped at attention in front of Beaulieu, stared at him from an interior darkness, and ground his perfect teeth together. Then he turned and hobbled from the building on that warm morning in late summer.

Rattling Hail appeared the second time while he was exercising his new service connected plastic limb. He marched and pounded the cement with his new cane down Vineland Place in Minneapolis. Near the entrance to the Guthrie Theater and the Walker Art Center he stopped on the sidewalk, hit his cane one final time, then he raised his arm and saluted with his left hand, the wrong hand, several actors leaving the building. His teeth flashed under the street lamp when he turned in a military manner, lowered his arm, and continued his march on a plastic leg.

Rattling Hail, the warrior veteran on one leg, wounded in the white wars, saluted the theater, places in make-believe. He saluted the blond children dressed in purple tapestries, back from building imaginative castles with sacred cedar and barricades on-stage with reservation plans, with the wrong hand. He must have heard the new world rehearsing over screams from Sand Creek, where Colonel John Chivington said, "I have come to kill Indians, and believe it is right and honorable to use any means." He saluted the voices imitating five hundred dead at Mystic River in Connecticut, millions dead in the path of white progress, dead with the earth.

Rattling Hail flashed his teeth and listened as he passed; he must have heard old tribal voices on the wind, from the oral tradition down the mountains, from the woodland and across the prairie. He saluted the voices from his past, the voices remembered in his blood.

Black Hawk told that the "white men are bad schoolmasters. They carry false looks and deal in false actions. The white men do not scalp the head, they do worse. They poison the heart. It is not pure with them."

Chief Joseph told that "good words will not give my people good health and stop them from dying. I am tired of talk that comes to nothing. It makes my heart sick when I remember all the good words and all the broken promises. There has been too much talking by men who had no right to talk."

Yellow Robe told that the "coming of the white man is no different for us than dissension, cruelty, or loneliness. It is a learning for us."

Kicking Bird told that he was a "stone, broken and thrown away. One part thrown this way and one part thrown that way.

I am grieved at the ruin of my people; they will go back to the old road and I must follow them. They will not let me live with the white people."

Black Elk told that the white soldiers killed Crazy Horse. "He was brave and good and wise. He never wanted anything but to save his people, and he fought the *wasichus* only when they came to kill us in our own country. He was only thirty years old. They could not kill him in battle. They had to lie to him and kill him that way. The old people never would tell where they took the body of their son. It does not matter where his body lies, for it is grass; but where his spirit is, it will be good to be."

Tribal people were hanged then, children were starved with their heads shaved for the missionaries. Tribal women were dismembered by white soldiers for souvenirs, and the earth turned to crust and the water rushed through the stumps down to the sea. Buffalo skulls and tree phantoms howl and scream on the wind.

Rattling Hail disappeared in the darkness.

When the theater rehearsals were over, the actors mounted their wheels for new parties under the blood soaked beams in the urban hills. Rattling Hail had saluted their passing in the night while other tribes enacted their cultural suicides downtown on the reservations.

Rattling Hail appeared the third time, as in a new urban ceremonial, standing behind a park bench watching the ducks feed in the autumn on the shores of the pond in Loring Park near downtown Minneapolis. He flashed his teeth, moved toward the birds, and then lifted his face and his arms in flight.

Rattling Hail appeared the last time walking through the new snow without his cane. Four months from the time he first hobbled into the American Indian Employment and Guidance Center, which was moved from the northside to a corner storefront location more convenient to tribal people on Chicago Avenue near Franklin in Minneapolis, he was walking with ease on his new plastic leg.

Clement Beaulieu and several volunteer workers at the center were watching the first winter snow from the storefront window. Night fell with the fresh snow while they talked in the growing darkness about the problems tribal people encountered in urban centers. The urban reservations were no better than colonial reservations for services, and the heartless governments passed tribal people back and forth like crippled beasts of burden.

The Last Lecture, a tribal watering hole for broken warriors, was located catercorner from the center. The corner door opened at the bar, and out stepped Rattling Hail, unbroken, on his new plastic leg. He stood at attention for a few minutes at the entrance to the tavern, marking his place on the fantastic battle line, his perfect teeth flashing across the street through the falling snow, and then he began marching without a cane into battle, toward the center on the opposite corner.

Beaulieu and his friends were sitting inside in the darkness watching Rattling Hail walk toward them. He passed beneath the streetlight, marching in a straight line across the street, leaving distinctive footprints. The heel on his plastic leg skimmed over the fresh snow.

Rattling Hail opened the front door of the center without hesitation, stepped inside, shook the snow from his coat, and spread his lips like an animal, flashing his perfect teeth once more. The illumination in the room came through the windows from the streetlight outside.

Then, in silence, Rattling Hail faced each person in the storefront, as if he were an officer inspecting his troops on the battle line. He stared at them, his black eyes burned in the darkness;

he turned the seasons that night in the center, ground his teeth together, and then he marched out of the building without closing the door. No words were spoken.

Rattling Hail wagged his elbows on his march in the manner of a trickster, and disappeared in the fresh snow. His new urban ceremonial had ended.

Crossblood Coffee

SHAMAN Truth Lies, the crossblood master of socioacupuncture and tribal trickster, interrupted an academic assessorization conference to proclaim a modest reservation economic development scheme that would corner and control international coffee markets.

The college provosts and deans at the conference were neither surprised nor displeased with the unusual proclamation. Tricksters were well known in higher education circles for exploiting familiar forums of instruction, revealing unnatural visions, and exposing banal dreams.

The shaman trickster earned his nickname in a television interview. "Truth lies in tribal dreams," he said, emphasizing the word "lies," and then he concluded that "white histories are nothing more than word piles," with stress on the last word. Reminded of these ironies from the interview, he allowed that it was "better to be known as Truth Lies than as Word Piles."

Truth Lies told the assessorization conferees that "the great spirits offered coffee to the tribes, and now we have the first proud word and the best beans, enough to take back the world markets from the word pilers." The deans sat in neat rows, stout fingers bound over their stomachs, like woodchucks waiting at the roadside for the racial traffic to clear before making a move.

The trickster had been invited to the conference to express a short tribal benediction, not a diatribe on fantastic coffee. The invitation was a throwback to frontier mission romances and racial overcompensations, but the urban shaman was not a native speaker of a tribal language, so he told a few short stories, seven in all, about the mythic world in the tribal mind and about how the white man was tricked from his illusions of power and dominance and then was taught to walk backward in dreams, backward right out of the country.

Truth Lies unfurled a small birch bark scroll. He gestured with his lips, in the tribal manner, toward the scroll, and then he circled around the microphone with seven dark red coffee beans in his right fist, an uncommon benediction. The trickster consulted the scroll from time to time as he told stories to the deans about the tribal origin of coffee, and as he talked he pinched the seven red beans into a fine instant powder over a cup of hot water.

First pinch:

In the beginning there was the word and the first word was "coffee," or *makade mashkiki waaboo,* a black medicine drink, in the Anishinaabe oral tradition. It was a time when Naanabozho, one of the first humans on the earth, a super trickster who dreamed in different forms and languages, spoke the same tongue as the plants and animals.

Well, several weeks after the famous flood, the first trickster noticed that when his earthdiver friends, the otter and muskrat and beaver, ate some red berries from an evergreen shrub, they danced and sang with such ecstasies that Naanabozho invented loneliness to protect himself from the shared pleasures of others.

He asked the animals to explain, but there was no language then for their pleasures. The trickster, an empiricist of sorts, ate some of the red berries, and as he ate he interviewed the evergreen shrub about the meaning of pleasure. The shrub shrugged off his inquiries at first, but then, when Naanabozho began to snap his fingers, roll his head and eyes, and wriggle his enormous toes in the shrubbery, the shrub revealed that she was named coffee, or *makade mashkiki waaboo,* the first words in the creation of the world.

Second pinch:
Great spirits created the species *coffea anishinaabica,* the frost tolerant low altitude pinch ground coffee which, until now at this telling, has been a tribal secret. *Coffea anishinaabica* thrives along the shores of Algoma, the Sea of the Algonquin, or Lake Superior. Later, much later, two other important species were created, *coffea arabica* and *coffea robusta,* in other parts of the world, but these species, as you know, are pinchless and much too sensitive to frost.

There are two simple methods to prepare *coffea anishinaabica* beans. The first and the most traditional method is to do nothing. You heard it right, nothing! The shrubs flower in the spring, and then red berries appear in summer. Late in winter, under a whole moon, the berries are harvested by shaking the shrubs. Sometimes the shrubs shake back and tell stories like this one. The berries are stored in birch bark containers with a fresh cedar bough. Some traditionalists show that one should pick and pinch no more than one bean at a time; the static fundamentalists, who walk and talk backward fast enough to lock the past into the present, teach that to save or store the berries invites evil admiration.

The second method is sacred, a ceremonial preparation shared by some women of the tribe. Vision berries, as the beans are named one at a time, are picked with ritual care from sacred shrubs grown at Turtle Island or Michilimackinac. Tumbled for several nights in red cedar water, the beans are separated and bound in birch bark bundles and suspended in cedar trees over the winter. In the spring, the beans are pinched into a ceremonial brew, and the hallucinogenic alkaloids released from this ritual process cause one to feel the summer in the spring, from red cedar coffee no less.

Third pinch:

You must wonder how such a fantastic coffee bean, pinched into a rich nuance without roasting, could be held a secret for such a long time. Well, the answer is simple: No one believes in tribal stories. We have hundreds of herbal cures for various diseases, but who would listen to tribal healers? What the tribes told the white man has passed through their ears with little attention; some are impressed with mythic form but not with content. Few people believe what we have been telling about the earth. The rivers are dead near the universities, fish are poisoned at the campsites, and the air is evil with pollution, evil enough to drive the cockroaches to the mountains for a rest.

Twice, however, we almost lost the secret to enterprising white men. Bishop Frederic Baraga, a small man with compulsive historical missions, tried *makade mashkiki waaboo* on several occasions. Stories are told about how he drank a cedar blend of *coffea anishinaabica* in place of sacramental wine during services on Madeline Island in Lake Superior.

Bishop Baraga, in one respect at least, became a tribal person, because his superiors did not believe his stories about pinch bean coffee from the woodland lakeshores in the new world. Notes on his experiences with the sacred *miskwaawaak,* cedar blend, disappeared from his memorabilia.

Then three white wild rice shoguns who had cornered the market a few years before, heard about *coffea anishinaabica* and attempted to shake all the shrubs for personal profit. Well, the shrubs shook back and spoke in the voices of their white mothers. The three exploiters were lost in a snow storm, misdirected by the talking shrubs, and never returned.

Fourth pinch:

Little does the white man know that once we shared the secret of *coffea anishinaabica* with the whole world. It was during the war, the great war, a time when coffee production of the most common species, *arabica* and *robusta*, was cut short, and instant coffee appeared for use in the field. Well, we supplied that first instant coffee from pinch beans, one more tribal contribution to the white man during his endless wars. Tribal children shook the shrubs during the war and pinched the beans for distribution as instant coffee to the soldiers on the front.

Fifth pinch:

You smile, surprised, a mask of derision, no doubt. Well, listen to this: The code talkers during the war spoke in tribal languages over the radios to confuse the enemies at home and overseas. While winning the word wars, these tribal code talkers maintained an elaborate pinch bean coffee exchange in military units throughout the world. Now you know why that coffee tasted so good on the front lines.

Sixth pinch:

Following the war, we saved our pinch beans, and then, with new economic schemes in the sixties, we traveled with the elders to the International Coffee Conference. But the conferees from the coffee producing countries would have nothing to do with our claim to a percentage of the market, even after our patriotic efforts during the war. So, with a sense of evertribal humor, we created a dance to the beat of war and brewed instant coffee at the entrance to the United Nations in New York. While we danced we offered free pinches of coffee to the public, a sort of tribal war dance coffee break. The hippies were impressed, so impressed by the effects of the sacred brew that they promised a brisk sale of our pinch beans to weird friends in communes on the coast.

Seventh pinch:
There is a notion that coffee fosters radical political discussions. Well, the world should consider the tribes as one enormous reservation café, more ominous with pinch beans than the Oxford Club in England or the Café Foy in France. The pinch bean *coffea anishinaabica* is the beginning of our best international revolution.

Since we were shunned at the conference and denied a place in the international coffee market, we have harvested and stored billions of birch bark bundles of *coffea anishinaabica* on the reservation. More berries are waiting to be shook, and soon, in a few months' time, we plan to saturate the world markets with pinch beans, a paraeconomic disruption of international coffee prices.

How, you ask, can we establish these markets? Well, it all started with the hippies, believe it or not, who shared some tribal economic values and introduced new methods of distribution. In the late sixties, like the code talkers during the war, the hippies spoke a peculiar patois and started selling our beans to romantic liberals all over the world. Europeans became our best customers for secret pinch coffee. Karl May Red Roast, for example, is cut and sold to tourists for more than a thousand times the original value on the frozen reservation shrub.

There you have it. Pinch seven *coffea anishinaabica* beans once a day into hot water, drink while looking at a tree, and your delusions of progress and domination through power will dissolve and you will feel a new sense of acceptance with the world.

Shaman Truth Lies pinched his last bean, and then he announced a ceremonial coffee break, time enough to sip his cedar brew and dance backward through the auditorium while holding out his felt hat.

The administrators at the conference on academic assessorization were so pleased with the entertaining benediction that they voted to name the trickster an honorary provost of the college of his choice. Truth Lies became provost of Kresge College at the University of California, Santa Cruz.

The trickster returned the gesture; he named the provosts and deans honorary tricksters, members of an urban reservation of their choice. They became landfill meditators on their own academic trash.

Four Skin Documents

PROVOST Pontius Booker was on his short but certain tread to lunch; he paused on the steps of the administration building, turned his shoulders in pain, pulled his thin spine in line, opened his plain brown coat, smiled twice, and then he approached me under the sycamores.

"Mister Cedar Birdie, is it not?"

"Yes, sir, it is *not*."

"Forgive me then," he said and cocked his head.

"Cedarbird is the name, sir, *cedar* and *bird*, the whole name, first and last name, *cedarbird, cedarbird*, metamask and metaphor, sacred and secular, in one unsevered avian word," I explained with practiced discontent, nevertheless pleased that he noticed me on the plaza.

He cocked his head to the side once more a pleasant manner that reminded me of small animals at the treeline, but there was no evidence in his smile that he was listening to me.

"Cedarbird came to me with the cedar waxwings on dream streams down from the clear blue window lakes high in the sacred tribal mountains."

"How interesting. You must be a rare birder to find a cedar waxwing in the mountains," he said. Pontius, better known as

Pinch Booker, his academic pet name, buttoned his coat, lowered his shoulders, and continued his tread to lunch.

Silence.

I had written that much, line for line as you read it now, and while it was being edited by the metaphrase editors, two invented Indians and one pretender from the Department of American Indian Studies cornered me in the computer room. The three were on one of their urban ceremonial meanders, a reversion to nomadism; they demanded to know what brought me to a computer terminal so late at night.

I was inclined to tell them that in addition to being a graduate student for the past decade, I had also been an informer, and a novelist, connected in mythic time with two independent computer editors, unknown to each other. One metaphrase editor is stationed in an arcane program at the intelligence firm, and the other is an editor at my computer publishing house. Both editors are private. The intelligence firm, founded to save those burned too much in the sunshine of public policies, edits my mythic stories about minorities and urban sun dance skins and sends them to special subscribers, and the publishing house publishes the same stories with additional descriptive material as novels. The truth is that there are three computer programs and three entries for my stories: information for the metaphrase editor at the intelligence firm, stories for commercial publication, and the third code is mine, a secret comment on the first two entries. My last words are sacred and private. I live in dreams, and dreams are close to secrets.

I told the metaphrase editors that myths and secrets are real connections, present tense imaginative adventures, sources of excitement close to the sacred, the real on the real. Political intrigues and competition are separations from the sacred, advertisements for future events, the mirrors that precede the images. The open world of fiction is political, but the secret world, the world of the informer, is a mythic connection to the sacred and a real event for me. I am the new tribal memories in the computers.

The three who had discovered me fingered their plastic beads in the computer room. Their breath was heated. We were surprised by each other that night. I smiled and told them the truth, without hesitation, knowing that the truth would be unbelievable. In a world of lies, the best deception is the truth.

"I am a novelist, a tribal trickster in the written tradition, and a paid informer for an independent intelligence firm that provides information to various business organizations, universities, including this one, and government agencies." I spoke in a casual but firm voice, and never smiled. Their mouths moved for several seconds in silence; they searched for a word, or bleat. Then, in close order, the three responded.

"Man, what is this, brother?"

"Man, what is this shit?"

"Man, you some fuckin trickster?"

"This is a new tribal word machine," I said and then printed their names, proud urban sun dance names, in neat upper case green letters, spaced in a row on the video display terminal.

San Francisco Sun Dance Code Names:

TOUCH TONE   FAST FOOD   TOKEN WHITE

"Now the real truth, man."

"The truth is that this computer time was given to me to do research, but research is too slow to hold the night, so I have been telling stories to this machine about being a crossblood skin and graduate student."

"Man, what is this, brother?"

"Man, what is this shit?"

"Man, you some fuckin trickster?"

In secular time I touched the secret codes and delivered on the green screen the first page of these stories, which are similar to the report for the metaphrase editors, less these notes and comments on the students who found me here.

"Here is the first page of the novel," I said, pointing to the screen. "The last of the oral tradition in electronic word processing."

Televised words wavered on the screen. *Provost Pontius Booker was on his short but certain tread to lunch; he paused on the steps of the administration building, turned his shoulders in pain. . . .*

"Man, I was there then, at the drum."

"Man, what is this shit?"

"Shit, man, he called you *birdie*."

In the past, when I first worked for the firm and wrote satirical stories with factual and critical details, the metaphrase editor raised questions about validation. "The truth," she demanded, over and over, "send me the imaginative truth about Indians in higher education, not the dead academic facts."

She insisted that "satire is not the truth." I argued that satire was one form of autobiographical expression that reveals who we are and what we have become in the white world. We are still much too serious about being invented Indians. Not satire as shame, I told the metaphrase editor, or the harsh control of social ridicule, but satire from the magical connections with the oral tradition. In his book *The Power of Satire*, Robert Elliot writes about a "mystical ethos" in satire, from ritual dances and tribal trickeries through word and phrase duels. Satire, not as a moral justification, but satire as a way to know ourselves in the new word wars.

I pleaded with the metaphrase editor to understand that we

were invented by missionaries and theologians and social scientists subsidized by the federal government, and now, in the cities, we are rewarded, praised, and programmed for validating the invention of the Indian. In that dialectic we are impressed to assume ownership of strange experiences: imitate data, live out theories, pretend our lives in beads and feathers, hold their mirrors for portraits and photographs, and serve as models, wilderness brothers and sisters to campers and hunters and ecologists. We have even been taught to resist questions about ourselves, about the Indian invention, because the white world has invested too much in the invention. But our languages and mood of encounters and learning are still open to the world, the tart tongues of satire and trickeries on computer screens.

"Send us the imaginative truth about Indians and save the theories on satire," the metaphrase editor wrote to me.

At first the metaphrase editor at the intelligence firm and the editor at the publishing house resisted the idea of satire, but with an occasional precious metaphor on mother earth, the two editors have not complained as much over the stories about invented Indians. Satire is natural, a trickster signature in my sacred computer entries. The computer has been a sacred tribal performance.

The intelligence firm considers me one of the best informers; their clients depend on my information. The metaphrase editor, wherever she lives, supports me and cares for me in the world. She celebrates imaginative information, reminding me from time to time to make use of mythic experiences and more metaphors. The best intelligence, she wrote to me through the computer, is *mythic*, yes, *mythic*, and then she transmitted this quotation from *Mythologies* by Roland Barthes: "Myth hides nothing and flaunts nothing. . . . Myth is neither a lie nor a confession . . . it transforms history into nature."

The tribes were never able to hold their secrets in oral stories. Now the computer holds the stories and the secrets in silence. The novelist N. Scott Momaday wrote that in "the oral tradition silence is the sanctuary of sound." The computer has become the new tribal sanctuary.

Metaphrase loves names, tribal names, and she loves to hear me tell stories about the students, such as Bad Mouth, Knee High, Fast Food, and Token White. Her favorite character is Touch Tone, the urban skin who wields a red plastic pistol filled with sacred water from the sand shores of Bear Island on the Leech Lake Reservation in Minnesota. Touch Tone shoots skins, an urban tribal consecration, but he never shoots white people. Metaphrase was pleased to learn about mythic racial divisions, but she does not like to read rhetorical questions. Token White was the only whiteskin Touch Tone shot with sacred water from his dream place on the earth; he believes the water cures tribal spirits in cities and calls back lost shadows.

Some tribal names are given, some are borrowed and dreamed and stolen, but descriptive names in translation are too far from the sacred to hold much power. Traditional tribal skins never told their secrets and sacred dream names to missionaries for translation; well, not too often. But now, we live in new worlds, assuming that bird and animal names are different and suit the tribal image as public invention.

My other name, the one on my birth certificate, crossblood and normal under a whole white moon in a public health hospital, has become a secret name, a sacred reversal. Not even the firm know more than my descriptive name. My birth name has become secret, and my descriptive name has become secular.

When some of us skins took on bird and animal names in middle school on the reservation, the white teachers made us write all three names a hundred times as punishment—the first, the descriptive, and the last. Those teachers must have thought tribalism was a disease that demanded constant attention if it was to be avoided. In college, when we were expected to be authentic representatives from the traditional tribal past, we dropped our first and last names. Urban skins, missing out on all the reservation name games, have organized their own name change ceremonies.

The San Francisco Sun Dancers received special federal funding to turn their names descriptive, asserting in a proposal that tribal identities are derived from words that were once denied in federal schools.

Blue Welcome, as a lesson, is a sacred name in translation. The person who bears the name is far from the dream, she is a senior lecturer here in the Department of American Indian Studies. Her name came from a name dreamer in the oral tradition, recorded as a last name in the new world, or the last world, as the old shamans seem to remember it.

Silence.

Uncle Secrets earned his nickname because he dreamed names that he would never reveal, or could never remember. Secrets told me about this "last world" when I was less than ten years into it—a time, he explained in a slow and halting voice, which we thought he might have learned from watching western movies, when "people are severed like dandelions on suburban lawns, separated from living places on the earth." He pleased himself when he could use the word *dandelion* in his stories.

So here we are now, translated and invented, separated and severed like dandelions, and living in the cities with the sacred in computers. We are aliens in our own traditions; the white man has settled in our past. We tell about invented lives; we even invent new visions and names as urban skins. Was the tribal world ever so different from what we know now? Who were the tribal apostates then?

Must we be severed from the old dreams and tribal visions to survive in the cities? Severed from sacred places where water is never cornered at the curb, where we once lived without measured time: when we became birds in the morning and turned back from white feeders; became deer at dusk and avoided the salt licks; became leaves down in a hard summer rain and showed our teeth, and then, dreaming about the past so much we became an invented past.

Our time here in the cities is not to confess our invented lives to white people in church basements, but to dream the tribal past into tradition. Silence and tradition downtown on the reservation.

Sarah Blue Welcome has separated from the sacred with names and numbers, books and quantities. She took up her first name from the Old Testament and turned to academe in place of dreams, theories over intuition, visions, personal experiences. She is ruled with words, not a sacred blue welcome, not a calm color on the woodland lakes. Tribal students shun her because she has no humor or trickeries. Separated from living places, she has turned her world around in words. She packs the living and feeds her machines and appliances. Touch Tone would never shoot her with his sacred water.

Silence.

My separation is no different, but more interesting now as a mythic informer. We all turned to books and machines, new politics and noise, when we moved from reservations to cities. Written words became the mirrors of our visions and dreams; we

lost our shadows and popular memories in the cities. No mountains without words, no water sounds without weather reports.
The common metaphors we share stand as simulations from our
past tribal states. Natural power has become a chemical word.
We are transformed now in grammars, not as animals and birds,
but as pronouns.

In the cities we are forced to be imaginative with no shadows, no spirit. Some urban skins take up the tribal invention to
survive, but not me, never. For me, separated from the sacred
but skeptical about tribal fundamentalism, terminal creeds, and
political spiritualism, personal power lurked in secrets and trickeries. Secrets became mythic connections. I became an informer
for the intelligence firm and turned to writing, secret creations,
writing mythic stories about skins who lived out invented lives
in the cities, those who turned to word magic and materials.

Sarah Blue Welcome, part political scientist, part feminist,
and an expert on the lexical loot from the Sun Dance, was the
first uninvited speaker at our protest for student control of the
Department of American Indian Studies at Berkeley. At tribal
events, uninvited speakers were never a surprise, but some were
more unwelcome than others.

Unaware that she was participating in her own demise as a
lecturer, she lifted the microphone to her enormous mouth with
one hand; her other hand was hidden beneath a small red and
blue blanket. The students were determined to remove her from
the department.

Blue Welcome shouted into the microphone; her voice
bounced on the concrete and brick, and shivered in the immature
leaves on the fists of the pruned sycamores.

"Let it never be forgotten, students and friends, that there
is the sure hand of a woman directing the movements of this
dumb little feathered head."

I was one of the intended listeners, part of a small gathering on the steps of the administration building. Thousands of people passed on the plaza the hour we were allowed to protest, but only a few dozen paused to listen. However, more students gathered when she raised the red and blue blanket, presenting a male hand puppet with a tribal headdress made from sparrow feathers.

"Four Skin is his sacred name," explained Blue Welcome. Wriggling her fingers in his stout head, she introduced her modified Tsimshian ceremonial puppet with leather bound arms and oversized plastic hands. Their mouths opened wide, and he blinked his brown plastic lids; rows of thunderbirds were painted above his lashes.

"Four Skin is the minimal tribal man, the man with no woman in him but these three fingers. See how his little mouth moves, how cute, crowing with bad grammar, just like a man." When she pulled her fingers out, his head went limp and dropped forward, reversing the drape of his headdress.

"This little fellow speaks for the last of the noble savages, the last inventions of the white man, not the woman but the *man*," she emphasized, thrusting her hand back into his head. "We are in the new world now, where tribal women rule the headdress."

Four skins hissed from the audience. White women came to the windows of the administration building and folded their arms over their breasts. The students clapped and laughed.

"No woman would have invented a male feathered fool to mimic as a hunter, but the white man did. The hunted, perhaps, but *not* the hunter." Blue Welcome chanted her words about men, raising the whistle in her voice.

Five skins hissed from the audience.

"Women did not cant their medicine secrets and shoot and trap animals for stupid felt hats. Tribal women are the sacred bears and vision birds now; we gather berries with our hands, not bad dreams about animals. We touch what we eat and return the seeds to the earth; bad dreams about animals turn the water sour."

Six skins hissed from the audience.

Blue Welcome thrust her fingers in the puppet.

Seven skins hissed from the audience.

Blue Welcome, like her puppet, is her own movable satire, her own race and vanishing text, but she is no trickster; we all agreed to that much last quarter in her seminar on tribal political organizations, because she cannot tell the differences between mythic connections, bad ideas, and theoretical separations.

Four Skin, she confessed, and she is forever confessing something, was her most permanent relationship. Speaking through her puppet, she explained in tedious lecture tones how she has been attached and separated too often, like bad glue, from parents, teachers, and men, "More and more men," she moaned. And then she stuck to women, moved to machines and appliances in time, and then back to women. Now she celebrates her human connections with a puppet. Nothing sacred, nothing lost in material magic.

"How about pets? Keep a cat and save the tribes," Fast Food shouted from under the sycamores. "Never, never a smart cat," she responded, looking at her puppet and thumping his feathered head on the microphone. "Pets and men need to be fed; puppets take nothing more from me than a few fingers and a mouth full of my words.

"Besides," she added, cheek to cheek with Four Skin, "puppets travel with no trouble and are better listeners. But to tell the truth, I might never have finished graduate school without my little Four Skin at my side. Psychiatrists recommend them; mine has two, one for each hand, and she uses them to speak through during therapy sessions." Sarah Blue Welcome smiled; she hugged and kissed her puppet on the forehead, nose, and chin.

"Four Skin," she whispered into the microphone, moving his chin to fit the shape of her speech, "tell all those protesters out there what ever happened to General George Armstrong Custer at the Little Bi Horn?"

"Custer caught it."

"Caught what?"

"Custer caught clap from a shepherd," said the puppet in a deep voice. "He got it from a mule who got it from a mule skinner who got it from a sheep who got it from a shepherd who got it from his mother. . ."

"Never mind," said Token White.

"Lost that too," responded Blue Welcome.

"But tell about his death."

"Custer was a juggler of sorts, you know, skilled at manipulating his balls in all sorts of motions, on horseback, in his tent at night, where his soldiers could see his shadow rise on the canvas, but he lost his balls, all of them," said the puppet.

Four Skin nodded his head, dropped his plastic chin, opened his pale pink mouth, and waited for the next question from his mistress. She looked around at the small audience, nodded to the skins at the drum who shunned her, and then she raised his breechclout.

Four Skin presented several tribal and nontribal traditions and inventions. He wore blue circles on his cheeks, beaded buffalo heads on clam shells, plastic bear claws, rabbit bones on a breast plate, breechclout with a beaded codpiece attached, to emphasize his plastic penile parts, and knee high moccasins.

"How did the white warrior lose his balls?"

Blue welcome shifted her weight from one foot to the other in front of the microphone. Her angular hips seemed to fold at the waist like a manikin. She wore summer shoes, open at the toes; when she moved, the arch on the shoes twisted and forced her bulbous brown toes over the sole. When she spoke for the puppet her big toes reached out and touched the concrete.

"Sure he lost them," said Four Skin.

"How, then?"

"Fine."

"Watch your tongue," said Blue Welcome.

"The mule skinner said that too."

"Never, never."

"Sure he did," insisted Four Skin. He turned his head and nodded four times toward the microphone. "Little Big Man took his balls for souvenirs. In the movie, remember?"

The audience in front of the administration building seemed passive, bored, unresponsive, compared to those at other events on the campus. The student protest was scheduled to last one hour, according to official regulations. Thousands of students were at lunch or between classes, but no more than a few dozen at a time stopped to listen to the tribal woman with the assertive toes and the puppet with a headdress. The tribal students blamed the poor attendance on the puppet.

However, across the plaza, hundreds of enthusiastic students gathered around a condom inflation race sponsored by several fraternities to call attention to birth control. "Join the rubber race and revolution," one woman chanted, holding a condom balloon.

Near Sather Gate, three guitarists, a band of student communists in red berets, a fire eater in mourning clothes, two evangelists, and assorted crazies were all competing for listeners and contributions. Third worlds and the time for skins, it seemed, had passed from student consciousness.

"What happened then?"

"Then, well, then," droned Four Skin, with his brown plastic chin extended, "Custer lost the war at the Little Big Horn because he lost his balls the night before. The poor man died not knowing where to find them."

"Is that the truth?" asked Blue Welcome.

"Sure is the truth. Custer lost his balls the night before the battle, but he has returned, you know, he has returned too much, resurrected now as women with blonde hair."

"So, that explains it," said Blue Welcome.

"Explains what?"

"Explains the attraction male skins have for blond women," explained Blue Welcome. She was certain the skins at the drum would like that line, but her attempts at humor were received with silence.

"What could be more pleasant and political at the same time," announced Four Skin. He turned his head from side to side, then nodded to the audience. "Fuck a blonde and fuck General Custer right out of his past without balls."

Silence.

The San Francisco Sun Dancers, a pride of urbanescent warriors with new descriptive names and new tribal ceremonies, and medicine bundles filled with vitamins and urban artifacts, were waiting with leather bound wands. The dancers were shore birds who preened over the dream drum; they waited for someone to remove the puppet from the protest.

"Shit, man, send that plastic blanket ass hand geek weirdie on relocation somewhere," carped Bad Mouth. Her brother Knee High was perched behind her in the sacred urban drum circle.

"Man, plastic ass," said Knee High. He mocked his sister and did tribal hand talk and warbled. His other talents have never been discovered; he failed his entrance examination four times before the chairperson petitioned his acceptance as a special student. He is best known for his wild warble; thousands of students on campus connect that sound with his lupine face.

The Sun Dancers hate Blue Welcome. Bad Mouth and Token White mistrust her sense of tribal humor and condemn the puppet as an obscene corruption of tribal values and the four sacred directions.

Tribal fundamentalists stave the world into fours, while the more clever and imaginative spiritualists remember the earth as a seven sided hologram: the four directions as reported, the earth, space, and a trickster who perceives and corrupts the sacred center to avoid numerical perfection and terminal values.

The San Francisco Sun Dancers show no humor over their urban spiritual wars and contradictions in the world. The meaning of their lives in the cities seems to be reduced from opposition and material magic. Borrowed dreams are clouded over with urban bromides and imitations of traditional experiences, but the rituals and the stories, however distant in sacred time, become the truth for the moment, simulations and spiritual distortions on the run.

Metaphrase does not encourage my editorial comments.

These urban dancers seek their visions in the concrete, in the politics of corners and containers. The Tarahumara tribal people believe that those who live in cities are "mistaken," said Antonin Artaud. The stubborn surrealist, who wanted violence to come alive and wounds to hurt in his poems, wrote in his book *The Peyote Dance* that it is not enough to be close in ritual and words with nature, one must be "made of the same substance as nature." The Tarahumara derive their "magical powers from the contempt they have for civilization. . . . there is no sin; evil is the loss of consciousness."

Listen, you can hear their drums. The sound is down and

contemptuous in the cities. Their clothes are dark. Black hats, black shirts, massive silver and turquoise, cosmetic western boots, solemn and sullen expressions, too serious to turn smiles. There are no tribal trickeries in them at the drum. That sound harms birds, downs them from magical flight, and there is winter and war and terminal darkness in the sounds of their urban world.

The San Francisco Sun Dancers are hooked to illusions from the past, a colonial tether, federal funds and government socialism, and the translations of anthropologists and ethnologists.

The tribal invention is so compelling that thousands of white people, lost and separated in the inventions of their own culture, rush out each night on television talk shows in pursuit of descriptive names, urban tribal visions, and dance in proud circles on the concrete with stained chicken feathers.

The wrath and furies of the tribes turn back on patent histories that were carved from romantic trees, single stave bows, untamed, wild, and balanced. We are the remains of the noble savage, wandering through the cities, with no shadows in our own comedies, satires, and thunderstorms.

In the cities we have become what we resisted in the past. A sublime invention, wild and clean, primitive and simple, but defeated warriors and drunken fools, prime bucks lurking at the treeline, natural ecologists invoking mother earth in litigation.

Anaïs Nin wrote about us invented skins in *Under a Glass Bell*, wandering in the cities, on a "slow walk like a somnambulist enmeshed in the past and unable to walk into the present." She saw the noble invention alone on the streets, "loaded with memories, cast down by them . . . He saw only the madness of the world."

The animals wandered with us for a time, and our madness made us perfect victims for television cultures in the cities. We are needed now as inventions, victims in the white world, stoic on simulated horseback, leather bound on a winter trapline, floating in a perfect white parade, beaded in the suburbs. Skins who spurn the inventions become invisible, imperfect victims. Those who boarded the urban transition trains on one way rides through patent inventions became proud planners, tribal merchants shipping new inventions back to the reservations. Nothing is secure but secrets and silence in the computer.

The energies of the earth, mornings and memories of the treeline, mythic connections with animals, birds, and plants move through me in dreams and stories. Seeds take the wind, cedar birds and the waxwings whistle. Silence is not an invention; there are no beaded thunderbirds, material separations, chicken feathers, or plastic bear claws in the computer. My silence is no invention, no swatch of animal fur to mark the passing of our tribal visions and memories.

There is some evil in all inventions and possessions. Praise no more apostates, no more spiritual ideologies and evangelists in tribal robes. Separations from the sacred, breaks in mythic connections, leave us breathless and shadowless as perfect victims in urban parking lots.

Urban skins know about the magic of telephones and televisions, microwaves and tape decks, but not enough about visions and dreams and silence. Silence. Secrets and silence. The old shamans spoke like the bears and the mountains and the cottonwood trees in the wind. The skins we hear in the cities are not shamans because shamans move in a mythic silence. Shamans hold secrets and silence in remembered stories; mine are in the computer.

The metaphrase editor told me to send more information on Doc Cloud Burst, the creator of the San Francisco Sun Dancers. The subscribers wanted to know more about his urban vision that took place on Wednesday, April 1, 1942, during the full moon of the fourth month, four hours before dawn at the coastal defense bunker overlooking Rodeo Lagoon.

"Man, what is this?" said Fast Food.

"Man, what is this shit?" said Touch Tone.

"Man, you some fuckin trickster?" said Token White.

I touched the screen and the stories were told in silence. *The last great war never reached the urban tribal dreamers at Fort Cronkite in Rodeo Lagoon near the Golden Gate Bridge.*

"Man, stop that shit," said Token White.

John Saint Peterson, reservation born crossblood corporal in the Sixth Coastal Artillery Battery, loaded and unloaded that sixteen millimeter cannon at the harbor defense bunker, but he never fired a round until there was peace. He saluted the sea seven times that night and became known as Doc Cloud Burst, the metropolitan founder of the San Francisco Sun Dancers.

Silence the documents.

Luminous Thighs

Language is the main instrument of man's refusal to accept the world as it is. Without that refusal, without the increasing generation by the mind of "counter worlds" . . . we would turn forever on the treadmill of the present. George Steiner, *After Babel*

Since the environment cannot be authentically engaged the self becomes its own environment and sole source of authenticity, while all else becomes abstract and alien. John W. Aldridge, *The American Novel and the Way We Live Now*

The Intercity Train to Cambridge:

Griever de Hocus learned from various tribal tricksters, from those who misinformed him the most, how to disguise and contrive the common world, an act of survival on the run, and the art of mythic appearances. "Paint the mirrors, break umbrellas," he wrote in *New Myths to the Silk,* an unpublished historical novel, "and reverse the most familiar worlds. Turn your faces out in a cold rain and become a real myth for the night."

Griever moves like an insect in a humid crowd; he leans too close to burnished thighs, pinches elbows. He chooses verbs like toxins for his ceremonial hunt and turns his head between fast paragraphs. Near the treeline, induced from his imaginative wordfires, he plots new scenes in stories about two writers.

"This novelist had a small car for sale," Griever told an educated man in the opposite seat on the train to Cambridge. The man smiled but held his book as he listened. "When I inquired about the actual mileage, he paused, pinched his nose, and said to me: 'Listen, mileage is a material illusion. The real world moves in myths and metaphors.'"

" 'No shit,' I said, 'did you write that in the back seat on the narrow road to church?' I leaned real close and asked him if he had ever dreamed about becoming a woman. Writers understand myths better than preachers, we both knew that much for certain. I kicked the wind checked tires in four directions. Well, later I offered not to tell anyone that he once owned that car. He paused for a moment, pinched his ear, and then he reduced the price."

"How interesting," said the man on the train.

"Not really."

"What ever happened to the car then?"

"Well, that night I drove it into the river."

"The river?"

"The car was still in his name," Griever explained, "and when the number plate was traced, there were reports that he had drowned and that he might have killed himself."

"How cruel," the man said and returned to his book.

"Not really. Tired novelists like to discuss their mortal existence at press conferences from time to time, a resurrection, as it were, from their own myths."

Griever slapped his thighs and leaned back in the seat. The train lurched past the narrow rural roads; stories flashed behind the hedgerows. Old words turned in his memories, quaked as the aspen leaves that never mend the wind, words that break from their stems before the seasons end.

"King's College Chapel, have you been there?"

"Of course," and then silence.

"Ten years ago I laid my hand on a perfect thigh there, in the back row," Griever announced in a low tone of voice, and then he threw his head back against the seat and stared at the ceiling of the coach. "Luminous thigh, never touched one like it since."

"Really," and then silence.

"Luminous Thighs, how's that for a movie title?"

Griever, a crossblood tribal trickster born on a reservation in the back seat of a plain brown station wagon, holds cold reason on a lunge line while he imagines the world. His father worked for a circus and his mother grieved, a new meditation practice that she said was a sacred tribal tradition. Griever, conceived in mythic time, is a close relative to the mind monkeys from China. He fashions new scenes from interior landscapes with colored pens; he thinks backward and stops time like a shaman, or so he claims in casual conversations.

"I can stop time," he announced to the man whose fingers had curved inward in silence; he slumped over his book, asleep in the middle of a compound sentence. His upper lip twitched and his nostrils flared in a wild dream walk to a natural, luminous thigh.

"For if animals dream, as they manifestly do," wrote George Steiner in *Salmagundi*, "such 'dreams' are generated and experienced outside any linguistic matrix. Their content, their sensory dynamics, precede, are external to, any linguistic code. . . . Language is, in a sense, an attempt to interpret, to narrate dreams older than itself. But as he narrates his dreams, *homo sapiens* advances into contradiction: the animal no longer understands him, and with each narrative-linguistic act, individuation, the break between the ego and the communion of shared images, deepens. Narrated, interpreted, dreams have passed from truth into history."

The trickster advanced to the next coach on the train and sat across from a tall pale woman with small breasts. She wore white shoes with leather tassels. Her lips curved downward, and her feet turned inward. She smiled and closed her little book of poems.

"Haiku," she said and presented her book.

"Fat green flies," Griever responded.

"Square dance."

"Histories across the grapefruit," he continued.

"Honor your partner," she concluded and clapped her hands to celebrate a haiku. She held a wide smile, her face seemed to separate, and her feet turned outward like two thin sheep tethered on a meadow.

"Call me Griever."

"Why?"

"Robert Frost lied," he said and leaned forward. His head bounced from side to side over the rough track. "He never was a swinger of birch trees like he wrote."

"How do you know that?"

"Because, I swing box elder trees."

"So, what does that mean?"

"Well, I was about to say that anybody who has turned down a tree would never write about it the way he did in his poems."

Her thighs closed; the sheep grazed inward.

" 'Robert Frost, you old birch liar,' I shouted out to him at a poetry reading once, but he was much too old to hear me then."

"Cruel American," she whispered.

"Frost told the lies, not me," pleaded Griever. When he

looked down at her white shoes his mood changed and he wriggled his fingers around his head. "But I do love to tell haikus."

She leaned to one side in rigid silence, retreated into her book, but when the train lurched on a sharp curve she lost her balance. Her head bounced on the rim of the window; her feet leaped free and wagged in space. Her wide white thighs flashed like fish bellies and her pink crotch spread on the rough seat, but she never lost her firm grip on that little book of haikus.

King's College Chapel at Cambridge:
Griever sidled through the King's College Gatehouse like an errant monk, with the wide smile of a trickster. He circled Gibbs' Building past Old Lodge and entered the chapel from Front Court. Inside, in the cool stone air and rich light, he counted cadence as he weaved between passive tourists and rows and rows of vacant chairs to the organ case screens. There, in the dark wooden vault, he extended his short arms, pitched his shoulders from side to side like a swimmer, and turned in a slow circle. With his head back, the roses carved on the wooden ceiling turned in the shadows.

Griever was prepared this time, his second visit to Cambridge. Ten years earlier, when he was on a special tour of academic shrines, he encountered two unusual women, China Browne and Lettice Swann, in King's College Chapel.

China Browne stood alone at the end of the chapel in front of the high altar and Rubens' *Adoration of the Magi.* Griever asked her to take his picture as he posed like an angel in magical flight, the tips of his golden wings touched and shivered in blurred light, but he did not have a camera. When he read *On Photography* by Susan Sontag, he sold his camera and closed his darkroom in the basement. He no longer collected or possessed the world on film, but he did like others to take his picture. China laughed when he borrowed a simple flash camera from a tourist and then asked the woman to mail a print to his academic address. Griever and China posed at the rail for one photograph; several months later he received it in the mail with an invoice for services.

Lettice Swann was supine on a bench in the back row of the choir stalls. She wore bright white shoes with recessive heels; her feet were turned inward even while she rested on her back. Griever reached to touch a carved cherub on the provost's desk at the end of the choir stalls when he heard a whisper from the back row. He turned and saw her bleached blond hair spread over the dark wooden bench like the hide of a small animal. Her hands rested on her breasts.

"Touch this one," she whispered and then pointed to a carved statue at the end of the bench on the top row.

Griever stepped over the red rope barrier, tied to control the movement of tourists, mounted the wide carpeted steps, beneath the carved cherubs and satyrs, to the back row of the choir stalls. There, at the corner, he pressed his moist hand to her sensuous thigh. The muscles on her shoulders and cheeks shivered like a horse down to water. The burnished thigh was warm, turned warmer; the carved androgyne rested on one knee, her head turned low to the right shoulder. His hair was bound forward and plaited loose with cloth. Griever stroked her wide thigh, which was thrust to the right in the high window light. His muscular arms pinched her breasts small at the post. One foot extended behind her buttocks, the enormous toes on the other foot, carved into the base of the stall, were broken and worn smooth.

Griever leaned against the dark wooden androgyne and with his right hand he pressed the "play" button on his miniature tape recorder. Turned to full volume, the tape crackled twice, hissed, and then the music, recorded by Giovani Gabrieli in King's College Chapel, escaped. The thigh began to glow with the sound of each anthem. At first the tourists took the shallow recorded music into their travels, but some of the children were not fooled, and in time a crowd of curious men gathered at the red rope to watch a torpid blonde hold her breasts and an ecstatic crossblood trickster clutch the thigh of a wooden statue.

Lettice dropped her breasts and Griever released his luminous hand from the androgyne when the music stopped, seconds before uniformed officials arrived at the red rope.

"Griever the carver is my name."

"The Carver family?" questioned one official.

"The Luminous Carver," said Griever.

"You, sir, are the third one this month."

Veronica Moves at Sundance:

Robert Redford

Sundance Film Institute

Provo, Utah

Dear Ordinary Bob:

We met on your Mandan ski lift two summers ago, remember? I'm the one who rode around and around on the chair lift when you were, as usual, three hours late for our appointment. In the end, however, the wait was worth the pleasure of your smile.

"Luminous Thighs," which you applauded on the lift, appears in several mythic parts. Here it is. Each episode opens with a close focus on the dark wooden thigh of an androgyne statue in King's College Chapel. Those who touch the thigh experience ecstatic heat, symbolic reversals, and mythic transformations. I told you on the Mandan that my imaginative stories feature crossbloods, and so, the characters here are tribal crossbloods.

LUMINOUS THIGHS
Film Proposal in Two Voices
By Griever de Hocus

Part One: *Gull Shit on the Lighthouse*

Lettice Swann stands behind the engraved flowers and lightning bolts on a new window of Saint Nicholas Church at Moreton in Dorset. Her narrow face is pinched behind a black motorcycle helmet. Lettice touches her nose and thick lips to the engraved petals, a perfect distance from Manley Powers, a turf accountant and novice church historian named after a famous general, who is on the other side of the window. She removes her black gloves, knocks on the window, and asks for directions. He comes to attention and smiles; his wide lips waver behind the engraved window. She speaks too loud, her voice breaks.

MANLEY: Wool?

LETTICE: Yes, Wooool. Is it near here?

MANLEY: Whatever do you want at Wool?

LETTICE: Lawrence of Arabia.

MANLEY: Yes, of course.

LETTICE: What did you say?

Manley stiffens, raises his head, moves back from the window, and expands his stout chest. Lettice, overdressed for a scooter, removes her helmet and enters the little church. Her orange eyes, fusion bombs on an ashen face, flash in the shadows of the altar. Like her father, she suffers from low blood pressure and poor circulation; she is drawn to heat, thrills, and fire, like a moth to light. Her doctor told her to be different. "Act like a man," he prescribed. "Deviation will cause you enough trouble to live a long life."

LETTICE: What are you doing here?

MANLEY: You're an American then?

LETTICE: Yes, how can you tell?

MANLEY: Your gloves, really.

LETTICE: My gloves? But I bought them in London.

MANLEY: Well then, who would ever know?

Lettice is nervous; she squints, looks around the church, and then examines a thin fissure on the inside of one glove. When she squints her pale cheeks seem to inflate.

MANLEY: New glass, do you like the engraving?

LETTICE: Nice flowers, modern.

MANLEY: Modern?

LETTICE: Yes, no colors.

MANLEY: Primitive, I should think.

LETTICE: Listen, this is not primitive.

Lettice is more confident now. She moves closer to the window and touches the engraved petals from the inside. Her fingernails are decorated with various shades of orange, colors of the rising sun, marbled like the endpapers in rare books. The colors are absorbed in the glass.

MANLEY: Primitive in the sense that the flowers are neither classical nor religious symbols . . .

LETTICE: Right, me too.

MANLEY: Then we are both primitives.

LETTICE: Not me, I'm an Indian. Who are you?

MANLEY: Indian? Red or otherwise?

LETTICE: Pottawatomi from Oklahoma.

MANLEY: I love primitives.

LETTICE: I hate civilization. Why am I here?

MANLEY: Looking for Wool?

LETTICE: Where did you say it was?

Manley posed like a general near the last window installed in the village church. Saint Nicholas, located near an old airfield, was bombed during the war. The final window, which replaced the shattered stained panes, was an engraved scene of lightning flashes and two rivers—the Piddle and Frome flow near Moreton. Manley owned a Morgan; he told her to follow close behind.

MANLEY: Lawrence died on a motorcycle, not a scooter.

LETTICE: The animals and birds are luminous there.

MANLEY: Luminous where?

LETTICE: Where he died at Wool.

Manley drove fast along the Frome to Wool and the luminous grave of Lawrence of Arabia. Lettice followed on her red scooter, and three months later she was married to the turf accountant. Manley, through his unusual connections as a bookmaker, found her a research position with the Lighthouse Authority at Trinity House in London. She mounted her scooter each morning, dressed in colored leathers, for the short ride to Savage Gardens where she compiled data on the bird shit damage to lighthouses.

Lettice studied bird shit stains by day and auras at night; she searched the city for luminous people. Several women glowed about the head when they laughed, but the light failed when they were silent. Then, beneath the railroad tracks at Charing Cross Bridge, she found a frail but luminous man. His dark street friends, such as they were, called him Torcher, and some sat with him to read at night. Torcher could roll light between his stiff fingers and flick small beam balls into the air; light escaped from his sleeves and shirt collar.

"Sawney Bean, the cannibal king from Scotland, knew about luminous thighs," Torcher told Lettice, "but I learned how to turn the thigh on whilst I sang in the choir at King's College Chapel. Actually, it was a joint choral with St. John's College. My doctor, you see, told me to be active for low blood pressure. 'Reverse the world,' he said to me, 'act like a woman and your cheeks will turn pink.' So I turned to song and now the light never stops."

A train passed overhead, and the abutment trembled. Torcher waited and then leaned back when the train had passed. His fingers flashed when he counted, when he gestured; he drew pictures of fantastic animals in the dark air.

"We were singing the anthem 'Give Us the Wings of Faith' when I first rested my hand on the statue. The wood was warm. We sang and my hand slid down to the polished thigh. In the middle of 'O How Glorious,' my hand was hot, and when I looked down, the thigh and my hand were surrounded by a blue light.

"When the organ stopped and the anthem ended the provost leaned over the rim of the stall and stared at me, his demonic face turned dark red, and his cheeks trembled in a silent rage. The little satyr on the canopy above him looked down on me with a great smile. . . . That thigh changed me forever."

Lettice abandoned her research on bird shit, neglected her new husband, the turf accountant, and gave her whole time to the luminous man. She lived with him beneath Charing Cross Bridge for several weeks.

Lettice practiced the anthems, and then she entered King's College Chapel with Torcher, and together they sang "O How Glorious" until the thigh was luminous. Lettice felt the light flash in her crotch, on her cheeks. She pretended she was a man.

Manley Powers, meanwhile, remembered vivid episodes of his time with Lettice. He pictured her when he watched horses exercise in a paddock, but he could not connect her in calendar time. She disappeared in his memories at the end of each episode, like an animal, separate from his sexual fantasies.

Part Two: *Mystic Warrior on the Ropes*

China Browne bound her feet for several months when she was a child, a pretentious reversal of her unusual abilities as a sprinter. Now a magazine writer with a whip hand, she wraps her divine pink toes in a silk sash once or twice a week as a form of meditation.

China, an urban tribal crossblood, is an ardent theorist but not a methodologist. Most of her theories, however, are developed from interviews and conversations rather than from imaginative thoughts or original ideas. Her imagination is limited by narcissism, but she admires, and follows from time to time, creative people. She pursued Griever de Hocus and borrowed from him one of her theories about differences in world views. Tribal children, she explained, have a passive world view because they now ride in the back of pickup trucks on the reservation and see the ends of landscapes rather than what comes down the road and over the mount. "Once we were a people of the sunrise, we rode into the light," she wrote in an editorial column, "but now we watch the sunsets."

Griever remembers with pleasure the first time he watched her draw the blue sash through her small toes. She allowed him to watch but not touch, peculiar meditation and pure eroticism.

"American Indian men have little body hair," she told an audience at a conference on tribal identities, "because they ate maize, which contains female hormones."

"What about corn whiskey then?" she was asked.

"The more you drink, the less you need to shave," she snapped back in a firm tone of voice. "The estrogen in maize makes some men better women," she continued. "De Hocus told me that tribal tricksters are androgynous corn planters."

China first met Griever while she was eating lunch at the Swallow Restaurant outside the Pacific Film Archives in the University Museum at Berkeley. Griever had unplugged a work of art, and the outcome of his act became a new part of one of her theories. "Men have no natural connections to the earth," she wrote in her journal. "Men are separated, and so they become tricksters to survive. Too much trickster in a woman is a man."

Griever pulled the plug and stopped the loud whistle from a teakettle that was on a hot plate in the center of a mound of boulders and broken bricks. This mound, placed in the museum as a work of art, was covered with soiled clothing.

China looked up from her fruit salad when the shrill sound of the whistle stopped. Griever was applauded by the restaurant customers but before he could take much pleasure in his act, a security guard grabbed him from behind; he had touched and interrupted a work of art. Griever resisted and threw the guard down; he wrestled with her in the middle of the work of art until the police arrived.

China, who had written about noise, cited state and federal legislation on acceptable decibel levels in public places. Her presentation was so impressive that the police issued a citation to the museum for noise pollution. Griever whispered his concern about the environment. China listened and watched him finish her fruit salad. His whole face broke into words; fingers, knees, feet, and the furniture within his reach moved when he spoke.

At the initial court hearing the museum directors argued that a work of art is not a form of pollution: "Imaginative noise indeed, but this is not the same as a cement truck or an unmuffled motorcycle." The court ruled in favor of the museum.

China wrote about the adventure for a magazine. The article appeared with photographs and a series of cartoons. In one a police officer pinched her nose, in the second cartoon the guard held her hands over her mouth, and in the last one a viewer held his hands over his ears. The morning after the article appeared, Griever rented a motorcycle, disconnected the muffler and roared through the museum around the teakettle. He was arrested and jailed. China arranged for his release on bail. Since then, she had followed him to two continents and had written several stories about his imaginative confrontations with the world.

China connects time, place, and common events to weather conditions and her various theories. For example, last month she ordered copies of *The Mystic Warrior*, a television film, to preview, but the videotape disintegrated in the recorder. An engineer told her that the tapes appeared to have generated their own intense heat and fused to the machine. He seemed to apologize for his mythic explanation: "*The Mystic Warrior* committed a video suicide." She never thought too much about the mythic or technical problems until the second copies she ordered for review were struck by lightning and burned. Then, when the film ran on television, a thunderstorm rattled the windows in her apartment and scrambled the romantic tribal faces on-screen. She drew a sash through her nervous toes and completed her review on time.

China does not leave her stories alone with an editor. She is paternal about her ideas and images and must be present when her stories are edited for publication. Mythic tropisms in her conversations, she believes, influence editorial responses to her stories. Her editors accommodate her common insecurities.

"What are the mythic tropisms this time?" the editor asked as he counted the pages of her review of *The Mystic Warrior*.

"What does that mean?"

"Mythic entertainment," he responded.

Los Angeles Times Calendar Magazine
THE MYSTIC WARRIOR
Reviewed by China Browne

Ahbleza, the Mystic Warrior and precious hero in this buckskin melodrama, a five-hour ABC "Novel for Television," comes to the screen from the disputed novel *Hanta Yo* by Ruth Beebe Hill. "If it is not of the spirit," Chunksa Yuha writes in the mawkish introduction to the book about an arcane band of mystic warriors, "it is not Indian." The film, alas, like the novel, is not about real tribal people or their cultures.

"I'm working on a film script," said China.

"Really," responded the editor who can read and talk but not smile at the same time. "Mawkish introduction, no less."

Ahbleza, the dubious tribal redeemer on a white horse in this ten-million-dollar television film, is a white variation of the old dualities of savagism and civilization, in which the savage is wild and static, noble or demonic. This theme denies the diversities of tribal imagination; nonetheless, the film reaches an eager and familiar audience.

The pretentious dialogue is humorless, and the peculiar tribal dialect is stupid. For instances, "Leaders listen and now they search for the truth," and, "Thirty and two of our young men killed." These racial and cultural distortions reveal the vagaries of creators and their audiences. There is some humor in this since tribal people are famous for their crosstalks with the white world, but what drowns the potential wit of the filmic characters is the parochial need to appear authentic. As fiction, the book and the film could be romantic satires.

"Remember that story I did a few months ago on that crossblood trickster Griever de Hocus?" asked China.

"Yes, the noise freak," said the editor.

"Well, Griever has a luminous hand."

"What?" he asked and continued editing the review.

"His hand, it glows."

"Jesus."

"My script is about that, about bioluminescence."

"Freak of the fireflies."

Ahbleza has a wild vision, enhanced by an untribal chorale, and then he matures on the screen like a mouth warrior, too much abstruse talk around tepee fires in the summer. A woman dressed in designer leathers chooses the hero as her lover; meanwhile, he resists violence and spooks his savage tribal enemies with an eclipse of the sun. Later, his pregnant lover leaps from a precipice to avoid tribal avengers. The hero and his warriors lose their center and hit the trail to the nearest men with "hairy faces," their first encounter with white peddlers on the prairie. Innocent tribal women discover calico cloth and their visages in hand mirrors; the errant warriors are debauched with alcohol, or "firewater," and dance drunk in the dark with their new rifles, or "firesticks."

"When he touches the thigh on a wooden statue at King's College Chapel his hand becomes luminous," said China.

"The human light bulb?" mocked the editor.

Ahbleza, the sober and virtuous hero, comes close to allegories at the end of the film: He rides his white horse to the top of a high hill where he is surrounded by savage marauders with wild face paint.

"I am a peace man," said the hero to his enemies, but no one listened. He was shot in the heart, through the sacred peace shirt that he had inherited from a traditional elder who told him, "Honor goes to the man who kills, greater honor to the man who heals." Our hero on the white horse was neither a killer nor a healer; he was a victim. This romantic fatalism is a myopic theme in histories and films about tribal cultures.

The Mystic Warrior, in the end, becomes the common victim of culture contacts, technologies, and turns in civilization, because white audiences better understand that simple message. The tribal hero could never be like Jesus Christ, though he is accompanied on-screen by choral music befitting a monotheistic creator. Ahbleza is not transformed; he is not a redeemer in the real world. He remains a romantic savage resurrected in racist themes to ease a white audience through their mythic fears in the dark.

"Luminous Griever could be as hot as the Shroud of Turin," China said as she leaned over the editor when he made a mark on her story.

"Our resident metapragmatist," said the editor. He shook his head, sharpened his pencil, and continued editing the story.

"Spare me the details."

"Right."

"This film violates everything I know about tribal cultures," said Terry Wilson, professor of Native American Indian history at the University of California, Berkeley. "The concept of peace, for example, connotes simplistic goodness and forces the warrior societies into a position of being evil.

"Warrior societies were a way of life, not a simple form of revenge. A warrior is a state of being, a ritual act of survival, not the structural opposite of peace and goodness," Wilson said in an interview. "The tribal world is more complex than dichotomies of good and evil."

"Listen to this." China opened her notebook.

"Dichotomies of good and evil?"

"Right."

"Who can tell the difference?"

"Indians."

"Teachers and preachers too, no doubt."

"Right. Listen to this."

"How can I resist?" asked the editor as he turned to the next page of her review. He scratched his head with a pencil.

"Court Circular, Buckingham Palace."

"Royalty in the first paragraph?"

"Griever de Hocus was received in audience by The Queen this morning and kissed her luminous hand." She continued to read from her notebook.

Richard Heffron, director of *The Mystic Warrior*, explained that the characters and events in his film are "fiction but not inconceivable." Novelist Hill protested that *Hanta Yo* was not a work of fiction. The surreal scenes in the novel and the film could be viewed as authentic by an audience unfamiliar with tribal people and cultures.

Promotional material on the film announces that tribal cultures are "almost all but forgotten. Today, there are few who remember the ancient songs and ceremonies of these deeply religious people who respected the earth, regarding nothing as more sacred than the right of choice. . . . Theirs was an old and spiritual way of life that was to end, abruptly and tragically, with the coming of the white man." Here again, tribal cultures are viewed as romantic victims of civilization.

"This picture is for a secular audience," the director insisted, but at the same time the film was promoted as an observance of the sacred. Heffron said that it would be much more difficult to make a dramatic film about tribal people for a tribal audience because traditional tribal people never "have eye contact, they never touch, and do not carry on conversations" like white people. He said he avoided the subtle sounds of tribal music in this film because the beat of the drum and the tones of the flute would not suggest to the audience the "emotional impact and sense of myth and grandeur" in a traditional tribal world. How ironic, it seems, that a white audience would better understand a tribal vision with the harmonic voices of a chorale. Heffron also directed *I Will Fight No More Forever*, the television film about Chief Joseph and the Nez Percé Indians.

David Wolper, producer of *Roots: The Next Generation, The*

Thorn Birds, and now *The Mystic Warrior,* claims that the novel *Hanta Yo* is "a masterpiece. This epic book makes every other book about Indians seem shallow and out of date." Such hyperbole produces income in the entertainment business, but not at the expense of such published authors as N. Scott Momaday, Leslie Silko, Paula Gunn Allen, Louise Erdrich, David Edmunds, and Vine Deloria, to name but a few distinguished writers from various tribal cultures. One word from any one of these writers would have made his "red roots" investment a better film.

"Griever de Hocus was received in audience by The Queen this morning and kissed her luminous hand on his appointment as British High Commissioner to the Council on Bioluminescence."

"De Hocus deserves you," mumbled the editor.

"The Torcher and his wife Lettice Swann had the honour of being received by Her Majesty," China continued to read from her notebook.

"Jesus."

Hanta Yo was published more than five years ago and since then the book has been the cause of more rancor in tribal circles than the rumored resurrection of General George Custer. Critics have exposed and measured the ostentatious claims the author and her trusted advisor have made about the authenticities of characters, events, and tribal behavior.

"I am Chunksa Yuha," the advisor writes in the introduction to the novel, "one of eight Dakotah boys to whom the old, old men of the tribe taught the suppressed songs and ceremonies, material suppressed for two hundred years, suppressed until now, until this book *Hanta Yo.*"

Hill wrote that the "American Indian, even before Columbus, was the remnant of a very old race in its final stage, a race that had attained perhaps the highest working concept of individualism ever practiced. . . . His was the spirit not seeking truth but holding on to truth. . . . This book abounds in rhetorical questions. But the rhetorical was the only form of questioning the Indian used; he never answered to anyone but himself. He conjugates the verb 'to think' in the first person singular only; he never presumes." Hill writes about people from her imagination, perhaps the tribes she would like to live with rather than the cultures she has studied. She is not the first person to homogenize tribal cultures under the generic name Indian, but her nominal metahistories precede written languages and the explorers and social scientists who misnamed the tribes.

"Her Majesty wore green sunglasses," said China.

"Griever, the world according to Griever de Hocus," the editor shouted, "what is it with you and this character?"

"Words and images."

"Words?"

"Griever unpeels words like oranges," said China.

"Jesus."

"Griever Christ, he delivers myths."

"Griever and David Wolper," the editor concluded.

"Idea and the image of the Indian must be a White conception," Robert Berkhofer writes in *The White Man's Indian*. "Native Americans were and are real, but the Indian was a White invention and still remains largely a White image, if not stereotype. . . . The first residents of the Americas were by modern estimates divided into at least two thousand cultures and more societies, practiced a multiplicity of customs and life-styles, held an enormous variety of values and beliefs, spoke numerous languages mutually unintelligible to the many speakers, and did not conceive of themselves as a single people."

Hill has also invented an arcane language that she claims was first translated into a tribal tongue and then twisted back again. This peculiar method, she explained, produced an authentic language. The nighthawk, for example, becomes in her final translation "Bird who comes at dusk and splashes in the air."

Allen Taylor, professor of linguistics at the University of Colorado, Boulder, writes that *Hanta Yo* "is offensive to an intelligent and literate reader because its purple prose is unable to either inform or entertain. . . . It is merely the latest of a long line of potboilers which take an Indian theme and use it to present a European viewpoint." Taylor questions the translations in the book and concludes that "even if one were to grant that it is possible to translate a work into an extinct, unwritten dialect, there is no reason why it should be translated back into another dialect. . . .

"In my opinion, the book is a classic of poor writing. It is repetitious and overly long, and it distorts and trivializes what it attempts to present sympathetically. It is a propagandistic work which perpetuates prescientific, romantic myths about language, culture, and American Indians which are better forgotten."

The producers, director, and the author appear to be enrolled in a new order of cultural missionaries. First there were anthropologists, now there are television movies to deliver the myths of the tribal past.

Remember, you agreed with me on the lift. If you can hire Mormon Indians to dance at dusk on the ski slopes and name your lift after the Mandan, then you can finance a feature film about crossbloods. Hope to hear from you soon.

Peace on you,
Griever de Hocus

Last Letter from Blond Mountain:

Griever de Hocus
Trinity House
Savage Gardens, London
Dear Griever:
　　Your script proposal is a rich slice of crossblood tribal kitsch.
We should talk more about your luminous ideas. Keep your
hand on the fire. The Mandan ride was unforgettable.

Best wishes,
Ordinary Bob

ABOUT THE AUTHOR

Gerald Vizenor, a mixedblood member of the Minnesota Chippewa tribe, was born in 1934 in Minneapolis. He currently teaches Native American literature at the University of California, Berkeley, and had previously taught at the University of California, Santa Cruz, the University of Oklahoma, the University of Minnesota, and Tianjin University in China. Before that he worked as a reporter and editorial writer for the *Minneapolis Tribune*.

He has published numerous other books, including *Crossbloods*, a collection of essays; *Interior Landscapes*, an autobiography; and four novels. *The Heirs of Columbus*, his most recent novel, is also published by Wesleyan/New England. *Griever: An American Monkey King in China*, his second novel, won the Fiction Collective Prize and the American Book Award. In addition, he wrote the original screenplay for *Harold of Orange*, which won the Film-in-the-Cities National screenwriting award and was named "best film" at the San Francisco American Indian Film Festival.

UNIVERSITY PRESS OF NEW ENGLAND publishes books under its own imprint and is the publisher for Brandeis University Press, Brown University Press, Clark University Press, University of Connecticut, Dartmouth College, Middlebury College Press, University of New Hampshire, University of Rhode Island, Tufts University, University of Vermont, and Wesleyan University Press.

LIBRARY OF CONGRESS CATALOGING-IN-PUBLICATION DATA
Vizenor, Gerald Robert, 1934–
    Landfill meditation : crossblood stories / Gerald Vizenor.
        p.   cm.
    ISBN 0-8195-5243-7. — ISBN 0-8195-6253-X (pbk.)
    I. Title.
PS3572.I9L3   1991
813'.54—dc20   91-50375